NOVELS by Par

The Feminists

The Inheritance

Marianne's Kingdom

The Devil Child

My Lady Evil

A Reunion of Strangers

The Shuddering Fair

The Scapegraces

The Studio

Reverend Mama

Moonblood

Dark Desires

Wreck

San Francisco

Restaurant

Golden Fever

The Wives

Grand Deception

Conspiracy

Woman of a Thousand Faces

The Devil Child

A Novela THE CROP

PARLEY J. COOPER

Order this book online at www.trafford.com
or email orders@trafford.com

Most Trafford titles are also available at major online book retailers.

Printed in the United States of America.

ISBN: 978-1-4669-9753-0 (sc)
ISBN: 978-1-4669-9755-4 (hc)
ISBN: 978-1-4669-9754-7 (e)

Library of Congress Control Number: 2013910210

Trafford rev. 06/17/2013

 www.trafford.com

North America & international
toll-free: 1 888 232 4444 (USA & Canada)
phone: 250 383 6864 ♦ fax: 812 355 4082

Dedicated to my sister,
Kathryn Cooper, and to
Carole Quintanar with
Deepest appreciation.

PROLOGUE

I am told that I must train my mind; that I must learn discipline. I must force my restless nature to abide an hour of stillness each morning while my mind rambles through the ashes of Clarke House and my hand scrawls scattered thoughts on clean white sheets of paper.

They tell me that I must write of Aunt Veeva, of the Covenant of Merlin—and even of Arhen.

When all of it has been written, when I have covered all the white pages with the horror of my past, then they tell me I shall be free.

Even my friend tells me that I must do this. Each morning she stops by my room and sits quietly on the edge of my bed, her hair smelling of lilacs and her clothes of soap and starch.

She has given me a bottle of cologne because I admired her fragrance, but I have not opened it. The scent belongs to her and to the flowers from which it stole its name. She has also given me many pencils. They stand with their sharpened points exposed over the rim of a blue glass vase. Without asking of my progress, my struggle with words, she glances at the pencils. If their points have not been worn down, she sighs and takes her leave early.

She thinks it is easy to write of past things. It is not. She thinks the morning is a good time to write. It is not. If I could write while I slept there would not be enough pencils to write with or enough paper to hold my thoughts. The nights are filled with ghosts, some dreaded and others deliberately summoned, but they vanish with the first light of morning and refuse to be coaxed forward for capture on paper.

Last night I dreamed of the ring of stones on the hill beyond Clarke House. The daughters of darkness were circling a basin of fire and shrilling incantations to the master of shadows. The ground there is unhallowed and vegetation refuses to grow. Even the birds shun the place, sensing, I suppose, the aura of evil hovering there.

These are the things of which I am expected to write.

But in the mornings I am drawn to the window sill. Beyond the yard, the wheat fields stretch away in a shimmer of gold to touch the river bank. The willows sway in the morning breeze and offer an occasional glance at the remaining chimney of Clarke House. The smell of the river is carried on the wind. When it touches my senses, I am lost.

My new friend does not understand the pull of the river. She has never hidden in the underbrush and watched a doe teach its fawn how to find food beneath the pine needles. She has never seen a beaver at work on a dam or a squirrel searching for winter acorns. She does not understand why it is hard to write in the mornings because she does not understand my love for the river and my daylight rejection of the darker life.

Write of aunt Veeva and of the daughters of darkness—and even of Arhen!

Arhen, it pains me to share you even on paper, but I must do it to be free. I must share you with my new friend, and she, unaware of her betrayal, will pass the pages on to the doctors and the investigators who have plagued me with questions since I, the Devil Child, came to their attention.

CHAPTER ONE

At precisely nine o'clock, as if by some prearranged signal, when the clock's hammer fell the first of its nine blows, the rain began to strike against the house; softly at first, but heavier and heavier still until it became a threat to the aged structure. The windows echoed the sting of the raindrops and the doors, pressed against their hinges, howled the torment of a backing wind.

Although the day had been cold and grey, the storm was entirely unexpected. There had not been time for the shutters to be secured about the windows or the drains to be cleared of summer debris. It was the same, I suppose, with the first storm of each year.

Clarke House stands in a grove of trees, far removed from the village, with desolate roads that never see the headlights of an automobile. The house has a surrounding wall but the trees grow on either side. Oaks and pines nestle against the house and offer protection from the heat during the summer months, but now with the sudden storm upon them, they turn against the wooden sides as if coaxed by unearthly will, beating their branches mercilessly at the command of the wind or some devious demon.

Aunt Veeva, snug in her feather mattress, waited for sleep to claim her, and I, although I am ashamed of it now, buried my face in my pillow and began to cry.

Rain had always frightened me. To be someday caught in it was my greatest fear, for I knew I would melt away to nothingness like the shadowy creatures in the forbidden attic library. Only the clothes I wore would remain as evidence that Lillith Clarke had ever been upon this earth. As the rain drew tears and each clap of thunder drove me further into my pillow, I became conscious despite my fear of a strange pounding resounding through the outer rooms and reaching the bedroom like a distant summons.

Aunt Veeva raised herself to her elbows and stayed motionless, listening. The possibility of her again hearing things in the night temporarily stilled my fright and brought me directly upright, my own ears peeled for a repeating of the sound.

It came again, deadened by a gust of wind, a low hammering from the outer door. It could only have been a summons from the unholy. My mind flew to the desolate hill behind the house and I shook with terror thinking that one of the place's captured night creatures had managed to escape in the storm.

Aunt Veeva, suppressing a startled cry, turned to face me. I knew without her speaking that she was going to send me off into the outer rooms with no regard for the danger that could be lurking there.

"It's the door, Lilly," she said, her voice too calm and coaxing for me to believe her sham of bravery. "The door," she repeated, "answer the door, girl!" She spoke as if a knock on the lonely door of Clarke House was a common occurrence.

"Let them go away," I said. I couldn't tell her of what my mind had imagined beyond that door, pounding its gnarled fists and waiting to snatch away whoever came in answer to its summons.

"Lillith!" She made a futile attempt to swing her lifeless legs over the edge of the bed. Movement brought a groan of pain, but she was persistent. She reached for the arm of the chair to support herself, determined to shame me out of my fright.

"No! I'll go!" I knew she would only fall. She had not been out of her bed since four Sundays past when a wandering gypsy had stood at the foot of the brass frame, raised his arms, and cried "rise," like one who frequently called upon some omnipotent being for favors. She had fallen then and had been torn with pain. "I'll go," I told her weakly. Even if the summons meant my doom it was no worse a fate than being left alone while Aunt Veeva lay helplessly on the floor somewhere between our room and the outer door. "No one comes to that door," I said, stating a fact we were both aware of in an effort to stall for precious moments of time. *Go away,* I willed. *Go back to the hell from which you escaped.* But the pounding continued, more urgent, demanding. "Who . . . who do you think it is?"

Aunt Veeva was silent, raised on her elbows still as if some muscle prevented her from ever again reclining. "It's Arhen!" she said suddenly. "I know it's Arhen. He's come home!"

My body turned cold. Arhen come home! She was delirious, struck silly by fear.

"It's Arhen," she continued to cry, and tugged at her blankets as if she were not afflicted by paralysis and would rise.

Even more frightened now, I persuaded her back against the pillows. I tried to mentally accept the homecoming of Arhen, my brother. I tried to visualize him pounding on the door of Clarke House.

"Oh, Lilly," Aunt Veeva cried, "your brother has come home! Hurry, child, hurry! He's standing in the rain!"

Torn between fear and the thought that Arhen might be summoning me to the door, I came out of the safety of the little room and into the vastness of the house.

Clarke House, no matter how familiar during the day, became as ruthless and frightening as the world beyond our walls when the sun set. Rooms which were intimate when sunlit slipped into the spirit of the darkness. The furniture was a maze of shadows. The watchful corners suggested evil, occupation by things that could not live by light of day. It was a house without warmth, living free of human involvement. If I lived here all my life, it would be as a tolerated guest and never as its mistress. The house did not acknowledge ownership. It stood as it had stood through centuries of Clarkes, watching them snatched away one at a time as Arhen had been and as I would surely be now when I swung open the great door.

The hallway had already taken on the smell of the storm. The musty, sweet odor had penetrated the carpet and rose to sting my nostrils, another of the house's planned attacks on its inhabitants. I brought my hand to my face and pressed my fingers across my nose. The smell of one's own body can be appealing when one is faced with unpleasant odors, especially when you know your body is faced with mortal danger any may not exist beyond another moment. I inhaled deeply and stood looking at the door, amazed that I had come so far.

The great door of Clarke House had not been satisfied with a single window. Instead, it had eighteen tiny panes that were inlaid to resemble a checker board. They were dusty now from being left so long to themselves. I wiped the dust away with the sleeve of my gown and looked out. The outside seemed of all but water. The vines hanging from the porch bobbed helplessly in the rain and were an outline of the darker blackness beyond.

"Lillith!" Open the door, child!"

Aunt Veeva's voice was far off. I had never realized what a distance it was from our room to the front of the house. If I ran for the safety of her bedroom, it would take far too long to prevent by being snatched up by some evil being the door might reveal.

"There's no one there," I called. "There's just the rain . . . and the vines . . . and . . ."

There it was, half hidden in the shadows of the trellis. It had heard my voice. It was coming forward. It would break down the door. I was lost!

I ran backward until I touched the wall, and was pressed there in the grip of the flowery paper when the pounding began again.

"Let me in! Veeva! Let me in!"

She knew Aunt Veeva's name, this creature of the storm. She was calling it loud and distinctly, summoning her to the door. It wanted Aunt Veeva, not me. Aunt Veeva, who could not possibly fight back. Aunt Veeva, who lay helplessly in her bed thinking that it was Arhen come home. Aunt Veeva, waiting, still poised on her elbows, still calling: "Lilly, have you opened the door? Who is it, Lilly? Who's there?"

I dashed forward, braver now, and screamed into the pane. "Go away! Aunt Veeva isn't here! Go away!"

Pressed against the pane, the flesh of its nose almost covering one square and two enormous eyes peering in from above, was the demon. Her face was wild, streaked with rain. Matted hair stuck to her skin like that of something drowned. She had truly come from beyond the earth's sphere.

"Lillith, let me in!"

It had tricked me! It wasn't Aunt Veeva it wanted after all. It wanted me, possibly because I had defiled the witches' gathering place on the hill. It had tricked me into revealing myself and now it would never go away. It would circle the house until it found an unlocked window or a weakened latch. It would tear its way through and devour me where I hid. There was no escape.

"Lilly, open the door!" Aunt Veeva's voice had lost all tone of patience. She was angry, unsuspecting. "I'm coming, Lilly. I'll open the door."

"No!" I suddenly felt protective, wanting to avoid Aunt Veeva's destruction for the crime against worshippers of the darkness that I had committed.

My hand lay on the cold metal of the latch. I gave it a quick turn and rushed back to my spot against the wall. As soon as the demon heard the click of the latch it turned the handle. Slowly, the door swung open and the creature stepped into the hallway and stood dripping onto the carpet. I could not see her face because of the shadows, but I could feel her eyes piercing the darkness and boring into my frightened soul, searching, examining her victim.

"Our Father Who Art in Heaven . . . . Hallowed be Thy Name . . . Thy kingdom come . . . Thy will be . . ."

The demon raised her hands and pulled the matted hair from her face. She was playing with me as a cat would a mouse, teasing, waiting for the precise moment when terror had reached its height to spring.

"Lillith! Who is it? Who's there, child?"

Hush, Aunt Veeva. Hush!

At the sound of Aunt Veeva's voice the demon turned toward the open door and a dim light struck her full upon the face. I was conscious of amazement through my fright. I had always thought demons like those in Grandfather Clarke's forbidden books, with the pointed ears and goat like faces. This one did not resemble the creatures of hell. She had used her powers to transform herself. She was no longer the demon who had stood outside pressed against the window panes. She was strangely beautiful; wide-eyed as if puzzled by her sudden admittance into the house of her prey. She turned back to me, concealing her face once again in shadows. Surely she would devour me now that I had seen her secret face. I pushed myself tighter against the wall and closed my eyes.

"Lillith?"

Don't speak my name, I willed. Please don't speak my name.

"Lillith, is that you?" Her voice was low, caressing.

She will drain my soul from my body with my own name. What an unholy executioner they have sent to punish me for my curious examination of their grounds.

"Lillith, it is Echo," she said. "Your mother!"

CHAPTER TWO

"Lillith, it's your mother!" she repeated sternly, and stretched out her arms as if to embrace me.

No matter how anxious I was to have it ended, to stop this fluttering pain of fright in my chest, I would not move forward willingly into those waiting arms. No demonic creature would take Lillith Clarke without reaching out and snatching her, kicking and yelling, and devour her against her will.

"Your *mother*," she said again, her voice filled with mock injury because of my silent denial. She put one foot forward as if to advance, but it remained there, poised, pointing directly toward the corner that held me. "Lillith, come to your mother!" she suddenly demanded.

"My mother's dead!"

The sound of my own voice raised in protest against the demon gave me needed strength. Screaming wildly, I pushed myself away from the wall and sprang past her through the hall door. My leg struck the carved table that held Aunt Veeva's prized Dresden figurines and they crashed to the floor and shattered into many pieces. If we survived this night, I knew she would never forgive me.

"Aunt Veeva, it's in the house!" I cried; though why I called to her I cannot imagine. She was willed permanently to her brass bed world.

Her voice answered mine in a shrill scream that resembled the panic—stricken cry of a wild bird, but a mere scream was not enough to stop this night caller. I saw the creature moving through the door behind me, entering the library and moving slowly forward, determined on our doom. I swung the library door closed and pushed the bedroom chair against it, bracing it firmly beneath knob. Except for Grandfather Clarke's room, none of the doors of Clarke House were lockable. The keys had long since been lost and not replaced. Anything that got within the walls could not be held at bay.

Aunt Veeva was sitting upright in bed, a position I had rarely seen her accomplish. The dim light from the kerosene lantern revealed her white face and wide eyes. "Who . . . Lilly . . . who is it?" She stretched out her hand to me, waiting, expecting the worst. "Who?"

"A demon!" I cried. "A demon that says it is my mother!"

Aunt Veeva gave an incoherent scream and fell back in her bed, babbling like a thing gone mad. When she became suddenly quiet, I thought she had fainted. I ran to the side of her bed, glad that she would be spared the creature's entrance into our room, but I found that she was conscious. Her face was as pale as the linen on which she lay. Her eyes were fixed on the ceiling, unblinking.

The demon was at the door. The chair legs squeaked with the pressure she was putting upon them. I could see that my barricade was inadequate. It could never hold back anything so strong. I looked about the room for something else to fortify the quivering door, but nothing movable remained in the small room. Taking Aunt Veeva's hand in mine, I held it firmly while we waited.

My touch seemed to awaken Aunt Veeva from her trance. "Lilly." She spoke as if she were unafraid, her voice more calm than I ever remembered it. "Go through the bathroom and up the back stairs. Go! Hide in Arhen's room!"

"But . . ."

"Quickly! While you can!"

Reluctantly, I released her hand and moved to the bathroom door. When I hesitated, whimpering, she waved me on.

"Go, child!"

I will always remember her like this, I thought. Facing the demon alone and thinking of my safety was a rare expression of her affection for me. Tomorrow, if I had not been found and devoured, I would collect what remained of her and carry it to the church for release from eternal damnation. Even as I made this vow I had visions of the ring of stones on the hill beyond Clarke House and I wondered which shrine of worship represented the strongest power.

Braving the dark opening of the stairwell, I reached Arhen's room, concealed myself in his closet, and covered myself with a pile of his fallen clothes. Since no one had been in the closet for over five years there was a minimum of human smells for the demon to follow. I sniffed at Arhen's clothes and imagined that I could detect the scent of him still, distinct, as clearly as the day he had carried me from the woods, the day mother had died.

A sound reached me from the rooms below, carried only faintly through the dark house. Pressing my ear firmly against the floorboards, I could hear more clearly. The sound was voices. They cut through the carved ceiling of Aunt Veeva's room and died against my ear.

Aunt Veeva was talking to the demonic caller. I could not hear her exact words, only the familiar tone of her voice. It filled me with relief and new hope. She was attempting, no doubt, to overcome the creature with the words of God. If she talked long enough and hard enough, she might save us yet. I lay motionless, the beating of my heart throbbing in my head. The voices below droned on and on, never rising or falling, but in a steady pitch. Aunt Veeva is not afraid, I whispered to Arhen's clothes. Aunt Veeva will save us. She will!

I listened to their voices long into the night, not daring to move my aching body for fear the floorboards would give out with a disturbing creak and destroy the spell of Aunt Veeva's magic over the demon.

How could Aunt Veeva have thought that it was Arhen who pounded on the door of Clarke House? How could she speak of the one thing more important to either of us than life itself: Her face had beamed with pleasure, with hope, not suspecting as I had that a demon, not Arhen, felled the knocker.

Without realizing it, I drifted into the world halfway between sleep and waking, Arhen's clothes keeping me warmer than my own abandoned blankets.

CHAPTER THREE

The storm had passed.

Sunlight was streaming into Arhen's room when I came from the closet. I went to the window and, defying Aunt Veeva's orders, pulled back the thin curtain and looked out.

Birds were scurrying noisily back and forth along the boughs of the giant oak tree, and a squirrel, having found its way into the garden through the hole in the wall, was gathering scraps in its expandable jaws. Beyond the wall, a man and boy from the town were making their way along the river path. I had seen the man before; he came every Saturday to collect the catches in his traps. Later, when he came back from the river, he would have a burden of lifeless animals pathetically tied on a stick and dangling from his shoulder. As if his own crime was not enough, he had probably brought the boy so that he, too, might be trained and inspired to carry on the animal murders.

The boy could not avert his eyes from Clarke House. Finally, staring still, he stumbled in a rut and pitched forward onto his face. I covered my mouth with my hand so that no one might hear my amused laugh. The man turned and came back to help the boy to his feet. He took a handkerchief from his hip pocket and wiped away the mud. This one will not catch many animals, I thought, without stumbling into his own traps.

The man suddenly pointed toward Clarke House, his arm was extended as his finger moved from one point to another. His free arm he wrapped about the boy's shoulders as though to protect him from the sight he was being shown.

I stepped quickly back from the window. It would not do to have them telling in the town that someone from Clarke House had taken a fancy to watching them from Arhen's window. It would start the whole thing over again. Besides, I knew what the man would be saying. I had heard it often enough while hidden beneath the footbridge, staring up through the cracks in the boards.

"That there is Mrs. Clarke's window," he would be saying. "And there on either side of the brick chimney are the rooms of young Arhen and his sister Lillith. The wicked son and his demented sister. There were the window is broken is where old man Clarke plunged to his death. They say the room was boarded up and has never been opened since that day." Here the voice of the speaker would take on a superior tone, hinting that he alone knew all the secrets of Clarke House. "There's just two of them left now, the old woman and the girl. The Devil Child, they call her. She's the last of the Clarkes. When she's gone the house can be torn down as it should have been years ago."

So the man would be saying to the boy. When his wind grew weak and his knowledge of Clarke House wore thin, he would begin with the deliberate lies, those horrible lies so easily invented by the hateful. All the people from town were hateful; they all lied.

If I were old enough to learn the secrets of curses and brews, I would see that they all died a painful death. I would spare my friend Mr. Thomas, of course, so that we could go on meeting at the river on Sundays, and I would if he coaxed me, spare his daughter because I know it would please him; but all the others—snap—and they would be devoured in the agonies of my craft.

I pressed my face close to the curtains and felt the dust on my nose. The man and the boy were still there, still looking and pointing, still telling and listening and inventing lies.

Before I could work myself into a frenzy and be caught by the blackness that sometimes claims me, I came away from the window and went down the stairs to Aunt Veeva.

She was asleep, snuggled down into the softness of her mattress. The kerosene lantern had remained lighted throughout the night. The flame was flickering from lack of fuel. I turned the damper and it gave a final gasp and died. The sound did not disturb Aunt Veeva. She slept with her usual peace, her relaxed face giving no sign that the night which had passed had been in any way out of the ordinary. Except for the imprint on my bed where the demon had lain, there was indeed no evidence that it had not been a usual night and that I had slept here and not in Arhen's closet.

The outer blanket was missing from my bed. I gathered up the remaining ones and carried them into the kitchen. I laid them in a pile beside the stove. They would have to be burned. The demon had touched them; they would be possessed by her smells, her evil.

I fried myself an egg and carried it into the garden to eat. The sun had already dried the top of the witch grass and was working its magic on the smaller animals. The contents of my plate went to the squirrel. He was shy at first, hanging back and examining me carefully before finally dashing forward and snatching the offering into his mouth. As he ran for the hole in the garden wall, the birds set up a commotion of protest.

To prove I had no favorites, I went inside and carried out some dried bread. I scattered it over the grass, and sat back to watch them eat.

Saturday was my favorite day. Aunt Veeva always slept late because the whistle from the lumber mill did not awaken her. Then as was her custom, she would read from her book until the day was half gone before asking for breakfast. I was free to run through the woods behind Clarke House. Alone, unwatched, I could run like a wild animal until exhausted and then lie by the river to enjoy its solitude.

No strangers came to the woods directly behind Clarke House. It was an unwritten law. The property, although it belonged to us, had never been fenced, but the townspeople treated it as if it were. This was mostly due to the tales that Grandfather Clarke still stalked his land, waving his saber and shaking his white mane at any who dared trespass. I had inherited by dark moments from him, they say. He was given to complete days of wildness and had once beaten a young man to death for crossing his property line to trap for animal furs. The young man, although no one can remember his name, had crawled all the way to town to warn the townspeople never to set foot on Clarke soil.

More lies invented by the hateful ones!

Slipping through the gate, I ran across the narrow clearing and was among the trees.

The ground was still damp from the rain. Here where the sun never shone, the pine needles were like sponges beneath my feet. They stung the air with their fragrance. The dogwood was displaying its first blossoms, proclaiming to the world that it would never again be used to fashion a cross. I tore away one of the petals and stuck it under my tongue. The woods were silent, absent of any morning activity. Even the birds seemed to have fled before my arrival.

I located the path my own feet kept beaten clean and stooped and buried the dogwood petal in the wet earth. Perhaps someday a dogwood would bloom here and any who found the path would turn aside and be lost in the thicket. I found a stick and jammed it in the ground so that I myself might remember the spot and tread softly where the dogwood grew.

Halfway along the path stands the lean-to Arhen build for me long ago before mother died and he went away. It was here that Arhen found me that awful day, gathered me in his arms, and carried me back to the house from which I had fled. It was here that I had buried my face in the flesh of his neck and confessed that I loved him more than anyone in the world. As I stand here each Saturday remembering, I look down the path and half expect him to come along on his way home from the lumber mill.

"Arhen!"

But the woods retain their silence. Arhen doesn't answer. He had long since abandoned us and may never come home to Clarke House again. I wonder if he knew that day that he would go away? I wonder if that is why I clung so tightly to his neck and confessed my love?

Aside from the wandering preacher who had not been told the tales of Clarke House and had innocently stumbled through its door with his burden of salvation, the last outsider I remember coming to Clarke House was the doctor. He had come on mother's last day, unsummoned, warned of her need, I suppose, by some extrasensory perception common to his profession.

The day had proven to go badly from the beginning.

The weather had been grey, overcast. A rising wind had blown down from the mountains and the sky had held a promise of rain before nightfall. The gloom of the day had been overpowered, however, by the atmosphere inside the house.

Everyone seemed to have entered the day in an argumentative mood. Even Arhen, usually sitting quietly over his breakfast, had been irritable and had snapped at Aunt Veeva before leaving for the lumber mill. After he had gone, the house was unbearable. The three of us had gone on sitting at the table staring at his empty chair, hearing still the angry growl that had so unexpectedly escaped him.

"The hell with you!" he had snapped at Aunt Veeva. "You can go straight to hell!"

I had felt that his words were aimed at each of us individually, at mother and me as well as Aunt Veeva. I did not know what had caused his anger, but I had felt it was too intense to be directed at a single member of the family.

Aunt Veeva had sat with her head slightly lowered. Her legs were quivering. She had never been capable of braving a reprimand from Arhen. Mother could speak to her in any manner she pleased, but the slightest cross word from Arhen could send her to her room in a torrent of tears.

Mother, as if she could escape Arhen's anger by leaving the room, had risen from the table and gone into the library. She had stationed herself by the window and continued to peer out as if she were waiting for someone or something to appear and save her day.

Aunt Veeva, who had just begun to be affected by the sickness that was to paralyze her, had begun to clear the table, forcing herself to hum a tune and pretend that the morning had not turned sour. But the dishes were stacked on the kitchen drainboard with enough force to chip them and the tune had slowly turned into a whimpering sob. The jam was left on the table and the oilcloth went uncleaned. I had still been sitting at the table when she had come from the kitchen, her face a study of anguish.

"Go to your room, Lilly," she had ordered, and had gone into the library behind mother and slammed the door.

From my room, then beside Arhen's, I had puzzled over the voices below. Aunt Veeva's voice had been highpitched and angry, and mother had tossed back her anger like a springboard. At one point, mother had laughed. The sound of that laughter had brought me away from the floorboards with my hands clamped about my ears.

The sound of a car engine below had brought me to the window in time to see the doctor emerge from his shiny blue limousine, his black bag in hand, and hurry toward the door. The voices had lowered, died with the ring of the doorbell. More frightened by the quiet than by the noise, I had gone to the door, opened it, and crept into the hallway.

". . . the shame of it," Aunt Veeva cried. "What of the two children?"

The doctor had spoken in answer to her demand, but his voice was deep hardly above a whisper.

"Thank God our father is dead. Thank god he is not here to witness this."

Mother's voice was weak. "You love them so," she said laughingly, "even the feeble-minded girl. You take care of my children."

"Don't go! Doctor, please don't take her!"

The door had slammed and there was quiet settling back about the house. The car engine started and died away as it pulled through the gate into the roadway. Presently, Aunt Veeva came up the stairway and found me on the landing. She led me into my room and sat on the edge of the bed, her arm around my shoulders.

"Lillith. Lilly." She repeated my name several times. "Lilly, there is something I must tell you that is going to be unpleasant. I warn you because I don't want you to give in to one of your spells."

I had anticipated her words. I had known when the doctor's limousine had stopped below and he rushed into the house. "No!" I cried, and covered my ears so I would not be forced to listen.

Aunt Veeva had pulled my hands away. "Your mother has . . ."

To prevent hearing the words I knew were coming, I began to scream. If they were not spoken, I would not have to face them, accept them. Aunt Veeva's face had turned crimson, her eyes widened, and I knew it was the same as if Arhen had again said: "The hell with you!"

Shaking, she stood towering above me, "You little . . . You must hear me out!"

Nothing is clear after that. The darkness that often finds me closed about my mind, I must have slapped Aunt Veeva because I vaguely remember the startled expression in her eyes. Then I ran down the stairs, through the back gate, and into the woods.

The *wind* was blowing hard and the tree limbs performed a ghostly dance. Every gust of wind through the branches seemed to be screaming: *Run, Lillith! Run, Lillith! Run!*

I ran until I thought my lungs would burst. Every breath brought added pain. I was a nucleus of pain . . . pain in my chest . . . pain from Aunt Veeva's unspoken words . . . her expression when I must have slapped her . . . pain of fear knowing I might be caught in the rain.

I came to the lean-to, climbed inside, and huddled against the trough bark of the tree base. The rain began then, but I was safe. What raindrops managed to get past the dancing tree limbs were caught by the top of my shelter. I brought my knees up, tucked the skirt of my dress about my legs and buried my face in the folds of my sweater. The tears were warm on my cheeks.

Then Arhen was there, standing above me peering into the shelter. His head was pulled down into a greatcoat until only his eyes showed above the collar, dark and questioning. Bareheaded, the rain had flattened his hair and washed bits of sawdust into his face. He held out his hand to me in a manner that said: *It's all right that you've been bad. Let's go home.* Then he must have remembered my fear of the rain for he removed his greatcoat and wrapped me in it. He picked me up in his arms and held me firmly against his chest. I buried my face in his neck.

"Arhen," I whispered. "Mother's dead."

He did not speak, but I felt the quiver that ran through his body. His steps quickened and he held me even tighter against himself.

"Arhen," I said, "I love you more than any other person in the world."

We came out of the woods and passed through the clearing. What gossip the sight of us would have caused in the village: The Clarke children, the wild man-boy and his half-wit sister hurrying toward Clarke House as if pursued by the devils who sired them.

I could hear the rain striking against the coat, hear the wind through the trees and the thunder approaching from the direction of the mountains. The scent of Arhen's flesh was strong against my nostrils.

Inside Clarke House, Arhen sat me down beside the iron stove. The room was warm. A fire was always especially prepared in the back room for Arhen on work days. It was here that he changed from his mill clothes and bathed before entering the front of the house, a ritual Aunt Veeva insisted upon. She had not forgotten his fire even on this unfortunate day.

I huddled beside the glowing stove, unwilling to leave my bother's presence. Oblivious to me, he began to discard the dirty clothes of the lumber mill like a snake shedding its winter skin, tossing them onto the washbin. Naked except for a scant pair of underbriefs about his loins, he took a towel from its peg and began to dry himself. I had never seen any male, even Arhen, in such a state of undress. The sight of his nakedness sent a shiver through my soul. Each place he rubbed the towel his skin showed red from it roughness. His body was lean and tight, the muscles of his legs and chest and arms hardened from his labor at the mill. I was fascinated by the design of his body hair, a diamond of blackness on his chest with a narrow connecting string that ran down his abdomen and was lost in the opaque covering at his loins. His legs and arms were also covered in a black down, resembling, I thought, the covering of some sleek forest animal.

Arhen looked up at me then as if seeing me for the first time. His eyes read the thoughts within me. He dropped the towel and stood with the shadows of his body dancing around him beneath the swinging light bulb. As he began to remove the covering about his loins I screamed and fled to the safety of my room.

Arhen had looked like a demon himself, caught in his state of nakedness by some power that neither of us understood.

CHAPTER FOUR

Mr. Thomas sat on a rock and let his pole dangle lazily over the water. He was not interested in fishing. He seldom even baited his hook, but he found pleasure in feeling his naked line pull with the undercurrent, making him, no matter how slightly, a part of the river.

As his head nodded and came suddenly upright, ending his nap, I moved off my perch beside the tree and walked around the log to where one of the townsmen had hidden a steel trap. It was obvious to anyone the way the hateful ones camouflaged their traps by placing moss over the edge of the water, or branches loosely over the mud, leaving only a piece of raw meat suspended above, waiting. I took a stick and jammed it between the steel jaws and they sprang shut, snapping through the rotten wood. Then, reaching down into the water, I picked up the trap and flung it far out into the river.

"You'll never get them all," the old man said. "Too many of them along the river. Except, of course, on Clarke land."

"I'll get them all," I told him with determination. I knew he shared my hate for traps and guns and all other devises used to kill the animals of the forest. "I'll close my eyes and will all the traps to spring shut on the trapper's own hands."

He laughed. "You still think you're a witch?" he asked, and laughed again.

I reddened, angered by his laughter, and ran into the thicket to escape his watching eyes. There I sat down in a circle of bushes and peered out at him. He always started like this when he intended to become serious; always some questioning little statement buried between two half-hearted laughs.

Mr. Thomas didn't believe in anything—anything openly at any rate. He laughed at wickedness at witches and warlocks and stories of demons that travel about under the cover of darkness. He even had the effrontery to laugh at the circle of stones on the hill where the practitioners of the unholy held their rites. His laughter was piercing, a weapon in itself, that always chilled me to the bone. I half expected it to produce lightning which would consume the both of us at any moment. He had laughed most the day I had told him I would someday be a full grown witch and would cast spells over the town befitting their treatment of my family.

I didn't like days like this. I didn't like to be with him when he went on about things he called reality and laughed at what he referred to as superstitious droppings of ignorant minds.

One day I had mentioned Mr. Thomas' name to Aunt Veeva. Her face had reddened with rage and she had said she had hoped the old fool had died by this time. They harbored a deep resentment for one another which was unexplainable and would never bear questioning. I never again mentioned his name in her presence. Our Sunday meetings became a secret.

"You know," Mr. Thomas began, "I got Arhen the job at the mill?" He was silent for a moment while I remembered. "Well, don't you think it's time I did something for you, like I did for Arhen?

"No!"

"Too many fantasies, that's your trouble."

"They're not fantasies! They're real! If you say they're fantasies again, I'll go back and I won't come to the river anymore."

"All right, Lillith. I won't say any more," he said. He settled back against the rock, shielded his eyes with his hand, and tried to see me through the bushes. "Suppose you tell me about witches and warlocks. About all those things your aunt teaches you."

"No! You're making fun. Just like the others. You're making fun."

"Fun? Now you don't think I would come all the way down here to the river to make mere fun? That's a long way from town, almost three miles. You're not worth that much fun, not when a man's as old as I am."

"How old?"

"Sixty-eight."

"You're not!"

"Yes, I am. Sixty-eight last July."

"I was born in June," I said.

"But you don't know how old you are?"

It was true. "No," I confessed. I didn't know how old I was, but I had an advantage. "Witches live to be hundreds," I told him.

"In that case I should like to be a witch myself," he said. "Do you think you could arrange it? Without too much trouble, I mean?"

"Witches are born. I told you that already."

"So you did. It's a pity. A man at my age would do a lot to be a witch since they live so long." He wedged the end of his fishing pole into a hole in the rock and took out his pipe.

He struck a match to it, and then blew out a stream of smoke that was gobbled up by the wind. He took up his pole again, and sat staring out over the water.

I always liked to watch Mr. Thomas. He was a beautiful man; not like Arhen was beautiful, but in a different way. He had white hair that always lay straight down on his forehead as if it had been ordered there and was afraid to move even in a breeze. His eyes were blue and his fingers long and slender and not half as wrinkled as his face. Sometimes he chewed tobacco, but when he spit he turned his head away, unlike the men I had watched at the swimming pond who belched the black liquid in any direction they happened to be facing. Even the way Mr. Thomas smoked his pipe was different. He would hold it relaxed between his teeth, not trying to chew the stem the way other men did.

Mr. Thomas was most beautiful when he walked. He would put his fishing pole over his shoulder and step out with a great show of energy. "See you later, Lillith," he would say when our day had ended; and he would stride off along the path, his step never faltering until he reached the turn. There he would stop and hold up his hand. "Keep well, young lady," he would say, and then disappear behind the trees.

"Lillith." He turned and looked toward the bushes. "Come out now. There is something I want to say to you."

"I like it here," I said, stubbornly. It was true. Even with Mr. Thomas I felt safer concealed in a bush or sitting behind a tree, watching him through some private spy-hole, always prepared to spring into an animal run.

"People just don't talk to one another while one is hiding in the bushes," he said. The wrinkles between his eyes deepened and made him look cross. "Don't be angry with me," he said.

"I'm not angry," I assured him. To prove it I had to come out of the thicket. I sat on the edge of his rock and rested my arm against his leg. "You see, I'm not angry anymore."

"Good." He placed his pole back in the hole in the rock and turned toward me, his eyes probing mine as if they were seeking to read something that was hidden there. "Lillith, I won't be seeing you next Sunday," he said, suddenly.

It was as if he had struck me with his fist. Never since that first day when I had stumbled on him in the woods and he had managed to coax me into joining him while he fished and he deserted me on that final day of the week. It had given *Sunday* that special sound. *Sunday*—Mr. Thomas—*Sunday*—that one break with Clarke House—*Sunday*—no chores, no moving under the watchful eye of Aunt Veeva—*Sunday*—the peace of the river with Mr. Thomas nodding over his fishing pole.

"It's not that I don't want to come," he continued. "There is a special reason. My daughter and her husband are taking me to Hugo."

It lessened the pain, but only slightly. There were seven days in a week, six others for him to choose from, and he had chosen our day, our Sunday. "That's over the mountains," I said, attempting to display my knowledge and hide my hurt.

"Yes, it is. Just about at the opposite base of that old mountain there." He pointed to the largest of the surrounding mountains that made our valley so remote from the outside world. My eyes followed his pointing finger while I fought to keep them from filling to overflow. "It's in another valley much like this one," he said. "But it's an ugly town, sterile, gone dead because the mills cut down all the lumber and destroyed themselves." He sighed wearily. "I guess you might call it a ghost town."

"Then why are you going?"

"I have to go."

"Will it take all week?"

"No," he laughed. "It won't take the full day, just the heart of it."

Just the heart of one day, and he had chosen our Sunday.

"It's to do with the trip, my wanting to talk to you." He wet his lips and I saw that his teeth were ill-fitting; they slipped together when he spoke. "My daughter Kathryn and her husband have been after me to take a look at the *home* in Hugo." His slender fingers played with the reel of his pole. "You know what I am trying to say, Lillith? You do understand?"

"No." It was our Sunday.

"Sometimes when people get older there isn't much of a place for them. The younger ones don't want you around so much as before. They sort of feel bad just sitting around waiting for you not to get up some morning." His fingers tightened around the reel until the skin of his knuckles turned white. Then he sighed again and reached into his pocket for a match. "Oh, they tell you all sorts of things—like it's best to be with people your own age, or you'll get the proper medical care. But it all boils down to one thing. They just don't want you around anymore. You get in the way."

Wicked, hateful people! When I learned the powers of spells, I would not spare his daughter after all.

"Kathryn—she's all right. Don't get me wrong. She was a good daughter. She never caused her mother and me any trouble—not Kathryn. It's just the way things are nowadays. Everything has gone and changed its values. Nothing is like it used to be."

I didn't know the way things used to be. I only knew they were not right now. Sunday was no longer such a tragedy. My friend Mr. Thomas was trying to tell me something and I felt it was important, one of those things you remember at night when everything is quiet and your memory flies over things past and you say to yourself: *That was important.* You fret and wonder: *Why didn't I realize it then?* I studied Mr. Thomas very carefully. Was that look on his face meant to warn me of some danger? Did his eyes reflect the thoughts hidden inside? Did he really mean he hated his daughter and would be glad if I should learn to destroy her with witchcraft? Was he asking in some way for my inadequate assistance? Let me know now—and not tonight! Please!

"But that is not entirely what I wanted to talk to you about, Lillith. There is something else. This trip Sunday is just my first. There will be another, and I won't come back. This one is just the teaser, just to make it easier, you see?" He knocked his pipe against his hand and emptied the burnt tobacco into the water. "Before I go off and leave you for good there is something I have to tell you."

A beaver swam along the edge of the river. At the sound of Mr. Thomas' voice, it slipped beneath the surface, slapping its tail to warn its friends of our presence. It is safe in its hiding place, I thought, watching us through the shiny surface, aware that I had sprung the steel trap and saved its life, but too shy for a thankful acknowledgement.

". . . things that happened when you were too young to understand . . . things about your mother and Arhen . . . your Aunt Veeva and myself."

A log drifted down the middle of the river, probably loosened by some boys further upstream. Unless it changed its course, it would strike the footbridge beyond the bend.

Then the townspeople would not be able to cross anywhere near Clarke property. They would have to travel all the way to the main road. Don't change your course, I willed. Destroy the bridge.

". . . you should be told . . . understand why Arhen did what he did. It's not my place to tell you, but I feel like you're my own daughter and it distresses me that you are treated like a . . ."

Destroy the bridge!

". . . it's unfair. You realize that. People like me, we're lost because of the changing times, but you . . . you can adjust to something beyond the walls of Clarke House . . . beyond the fantasies . . ."

Enough time had passed. The current must have caused the log to swerve. The bridge had been saved. People could continue crossing on the footbridge so close to our property line. It was unfair, utterly unfair.

". . . in bondage to that selfish . . . Arhen tried to overcome . . . He understood near the end . . . why can't you? Your spells . . . you're not really possessed, you know that down deep inside. It's merely a physical ailment. You're not the only child who suffers from such fits. You need proper . . ."

Last night the demon's face had shown fear. Perhaps demons, too, have those moments when they are struck by the grinding pain of fright. With her face pressed so close to the glass panes, her eyes glaring through the tiny squares, I had almost felt pity, pity for that creature Aunt Veeva had conquered.

"Lillith! You're not listening!"

Mr. Thomas' face was a maze of deep wrinkles, each running into the other until they were lost in his growth of white hair. His blue eyes blazed when he was angry. They were blazing now.

"You're not listening!" he repeated. "You haven't heard a word I've said."

"Yes, I have," I lied. I didn't like this day. Everything was wrong. It was like that other day when I had lost my mother. Mr. Thomas had become serious and I could no longer run to the bushes without offending him. Besides, some unexplainable feeling held me firm on the rock at his feet, staring into his eyes, pretending I cared and wanted to cling to each word his soundless lips had uttered.

"There are no *demons!*"

It was as if he had shaken my senses. Everything became clearly visible. I leaped to my feet, prepared, I fear, to strike out at him. "There are! There are!" I screamed.

He grabbed me, clutching my shoulders between his powerful hands, and shook me violently. "No! Say there are no demons! Say it! Have this done with once and for all!"

If there were no demons, then there were no witches or women with secret powers. If such women did not exist, then what was I! An ugly half-wit who lived in Clarke House. A frightened, ugly girl whom people pointed at from the river path and made dirty jokes about. "There are demons!" I screamed. "There are! I've seen them!"

"No! There are no demons! There are no witches or warlocks! There are none!"

I tore away from his grasp and ran into the woods.

"Lillith, please!" His voice followed me, found me behind the trees and hid with me under an umbrella of ferns. "Lillith!"

I could see him from where I hid. He had risen from the rock and was looking after me. The sunlight was glistening off his white head. "Lillith, come back. Please come back and listen to reason."

When I refused to answer, he bowed his head. After a moment, he gathered up his fishing pole and put it over his shoulder. "See you later, Lillith," he said; and stepped out down the path, his stride slower than usual, his white head hunched down inside his shoulders. He did not stop at the bend in the path; he did not turn and call: Keep well, young lady. He just kept on walking around the bend and out of sight.

I crawled out from beneath the ferns and was taken with the urge to run after him, but I was afraid. We were no longer within the limits of Clarke property. He had managed to draw me outside, each Sunday edging me further away from the security of the familiar woods. I turned and ran, and didn't stop until I reached the structure Arhen had built against the base of a tree, my lean-to. I stood puffing against its side, my heart pounding within my chest as if it would break through.

"Oh, Mr. Thomas," I cried. "Must I lose you, too? Don't go to Hugo. Don't even go the first time. Come home with me to Clarke House. I'll hide you in Arhen's room. We won't tell Aunt Veeva. She'll never know you are there. We can fish on Sundays. We can roam through the woods and watch the animals. Come to Clarke House. Come and you'll see that there truly are demons. You'll believe me then. You will."

I knew he would see me again before he went away for good; before they sent him away to a *home*. I would ask him then, I decided. In the meantime, I would make room for him at Clarke House. Perhaps Arhen's room. Perhaps my old room. It could be his now. Instead of his luring me away from Clarke House, I would offer him safety behind its walls.

I hope his daughter suffers the most when my magic arts bring destruction to the town. I hope she shivers and turns old and that her husband throws her out into the cold because he hates old people. I hope she slithers around on the ground like a snake and people come and grind her into the dust with their boots.

I hope Aunt Veeva teaches me the arts of darkness soon. I feel so helpless without knowledge.

CHAPTER FIVE

A unt Veeva had raised her night shade and was staring out into the garden. As I entered the gate, she raised her hand and waved weakly. Feeling ashamed for having neglected her, I waved in return and hurried to the kitchen.

I prepared her breakfast, a poached egg and two pieces of dry toast, and carried them in to her. She forced a wistful smile and attempted to firm the pillows at her back.

"The woods again?" she asked softly. "You mustn't go too far from the house, remember that. You know what may happen when I am not there to protect you."

"I know," I told here, "but the woods are safe."

"Safe, are they?" She spooned a bit of egg into her mouth and chewed quietly for a moment. "Just be on your guard," she continued. "There is no completely safe place for a Clarke. Not now. You know what they did to Arhen. They hate us, you and me. We are outcasts."

"I am careful," I assured her, and then because I knew she liked to hear such things: "The trapper from the town passed on the river road with a boy. The boy fell in the mud. It was very funny." As I related the incident, I somehow lost the humor.

"I should have liked to see that," she said. "Did he hurt himself? I hope he hurt himself dreadfully. A few accidents and they might abandon that road altogether."

"I'm sure he did," I lied. "The man cleaned away the mud with his handkerchief and the two of them stared at Clarke House. The man pointed out the rooms above." I raised my eyes to indicate the rooms above hers.

She spooned more of the egg into her mouth and lay watching me as she chewed. "Still pointing and whispering," she said tonelessly. "Still shaking in their ignorant souls at the sight of Clarke House. Someday they will see the inside. When we are gone. When Arhen comes home and takes us away. They can tear down the house brick by brick and have their peace."

"No!" My loud protest startled her. Even I didn't know if I was protesting the house being defiled or rejecting the thought of Arhen coming home.

"Don't be a stupid girl, Lillith," she said. "Someday this old house is going to crumble about our heads. Already I can hear rain falling into the rooms above. At night the owls hoot there and I suppose it has become a home for the bats." She sighed. "The house is already a ruin. Arhen has to come home soon before it tumbles and buries us beneath."

"The owls are just in grandfather's room," I told her. "They came through the broken window. I'll get some boards and nail them over the cracks."

"I forbid it!" She pushed her plate aside. "That room has not been opened in almost eleven years, and it won't be opened as long as I'm alive. Do you understand? My father's room is never to be opened."

I nodded in agreement, tried to force a smile and attempted to turn the conversation.

But she persisted. "The belongings of the dead should be left alone. They are not for prying eyes." She pulled herself up on her pillows. "Father lived almost entirely in that room the last three years before he left us. There is much of him still there. Sometimes I imagine him still walking above me at nights. Of course, it is only the creaking of the old floorboards."

I picked up her plate and sat with it resting on my lap. "Tell me about the demon," I suddenly asked.

She looked at me severely with the echo of my question hanging in the air between us. Her expression told me she thought I was an unworthy listener. "She went away," she said flatly. "I don't think she will bother us again—not ever again."

"What did you say to her?"

"Magic talk. You wouldn't understand such things. Not yet."

"Did you read to her from the Bible?"

"I dare say I did." She glanced at the impressive old volume lying on her blankets. "It can turn away the gravest of dangers, Lilly. Someday I will teach you to read the Bible."

"I can already read," I reminded her.

"But the Bible is more difficult than the books on witchcraft. Each passage has to be read and reread and then examined from all angles."

"Could the demon read the Bible?"

"I doubt that she ever tried," Aunt Veeva remarked. "That one knew nothing but wickedness."

"Didn't she look for me at all?" I was caught again, caught by the memory of the demon stalking through the library door behind me.

Aunt Veeva turned her head and looked me straight in the eyes, probing. "Did you listen from the stairs? If you did I will see that she comes back. I'll tell her where you hide."

"No!" I was horror-stricken. "I couldn't hear," I assured her. "I hid in Arhen's closet, and I couldn't hear!"

She appeared satisfied. "Enough of this talk of demons," she finally said wearily. "Go to the gate and collect the basket before some dog helps itself again." She adjusted her coverlets, a sign that our morning chat had come to an end and she wanted to be left in peace until lunch time. "After you put the groceries away, go up to Arhen's room and make sure you left everything as it was."

"Yes, Aunt Veeva." I rose and moved to the door. "Have a good day."

"A good day," she echoed. "As if one day could be any different than another."

I never went into the town.

Through some arrangement of Aunt Veeva's, the local store delivered our groceries to the front gate each week. They placed them in the wooden shelter that at one time had housed a statue of a saint, long since stolen by some village pranksters. It was my duty to retrieve the basket as soon as the delivery boy had departed. One day I had been late and a dog had scattered the vegetables about the road in his search for our weekly meat. That week we had eaten only bread and vegetables, and Aunt Veeva blaming me for my tardiness in collecting the basket, had complained of pains in her bones from such deficient meals. As for myself, I was perfectly satisfied to forgo the meat in our diet.

The delivery boy was late today. I sat for almost an hour with my back pressed against the rough wood of the gate. When he did come, he came quietly, easing his feet over the loose gravel and running after he had deposited the basket. I pressed my eye to a crack in the boards and watched him scurry out of sight. Then I pushed the heavy gate open and snatched the basket inside. It was heavy today; every third week the grocer added a sack of sugar and a tin of lard to our order. He had forgotten one week and Aunt Veeva had written a long scrawling note for me to leave with the money. The next week there had been a shaky note of apology and two extra pounds of sugar which we were not charged for.

Aunt Veeva lost few battles with the tradesmen. The only defeat I am aware of was the electric power company. As a result of one of her notes the power to Clarke House had been disconnected and I had been force to search the attic and basement for kerosene lanterns and to leave a note in the basket requesting the grocer to *please* obtain fuel and add it to our weekly deliveries. Aunt Veeva disliked mention of electricity or utility companies of any sort.

Clarke House is menacing from any angle, but I think it looks most frightening as seen from the front gate. I often wonder if some past Clarke had planned it so as to scare away uninvited guests.

The house sits like a bloated monster, the long narrow porch that runs the length of the front resembling an open jaw, the pillars with the overhanging vines its teeth, the chimney its nose and the windows above its watchful eyes.

Aunt Veeva says the house was once ablaze with lights. People came from miles around to attend parties at Clarke House. They would arrive in the finery, the boys and girls from the best families, and there would be laughter and gaiety. That had been when mother and Aunt Veeva had been young girls; before Grandfather Clarke became discontented with pacing about his room and dove through the window. After his death, the house lost its spirit for parties. Aunt Veeva hid herself away inside and the young part of her had died with the house.

What a grand sight it must have been in those earlier days, the envy of the townspeople and not the butt of their hate and whispered lies. I carried the basket into the kitchen and placed the goods on the shelves. Then I washed my hands with lye soap until the skin turned red; it always seemed dangerous to me to touch things that the townspeople might have handled. Their ill-wishes could affect the food. Is that one of my sillinesses? Or am I beginning to rely on special sensitivity acquired by age?

Either way, there was no need in taking chances. I would cook everything twice as long as necessary to make sure all germs were destroyed.

Maybe.

Aunt Veeva's stomach is remarkably sensitive.

Arhen's room was different from any other room in the house. Since he had contact with the world beyond our walls, his room became a carnival of foreign objects brought home from weekend trips. His bureau also holds a gold-framed photograph of a girl from the town. She is smiling, giving the room a timid cheer. I don't think of her as one of the hateful ones, but I sometimes stand before the mirror and compare myself to her photograph. I have never managed a smile as captivating as hers, and that is, I think, because I do not understand her reason for smiling. If I ever learn the deadly art of magic and spells and cast my curse over the town, I worry that I will not be able to save her since I don't know her name.

A large doll sits beside her photograph. It has buttons for eyes and hair made of tobacco-colored thread. Its clothes are made of potato sacking and its crown of silver with inset marbles. It is ugly, but I have affection for it. Arhen brought it to me from one of his trips. It looks misplaced beside the photograph of the girl, but I leave it there because that is where Arhen set it and it should not be moved.

In the corner, half-hidden under the bed, sits the unusual pair of shoes with the steel spikes in the soles. Arhen had worn them to the mill each day, explaining that they helped him to retain his balance when he leaped from one log to another in the mill pond. "You'll have to come and watch me someday, little sister," he had said, and I had been horrified at anything so brazen.

Secretly, I had always wanted to follow him to the mill, hide behind the embankment, and watch him jump from log to log, guiding them to the grinding jaws of the steel saws. But I contented myself with listening to his tales of life at the lumber mill. I would sit and clean his boots of the red clay while he spoke of making lumber from trees, of pulp from scrap, and of paper from pulp. He never tired of telling me of the mill's magic, and I was a willing listener, although Aunt Veeva said that girls should not be interested in such masculine occupations.

During the day when Arhen was at work, I would watch the sparks leaping into the air from the cone-shaped spire where the waste was burned, knowing that Arhen was somewhere beneath its smoke, leaping around on the logs, proving Aunt Veeva wrong in her belief that Clarkes were not meant to live beyond the walls of our house. During those days I had begun to believe that I, too, might find a place outside.

But Arhen had lost his job when the trouble had started. He had settled back into life at Clarke House, dark and moody, spending most of his time within his room.

Aunt Veeva had proven her point.

Arhen had removed the heavy velvet drapes that covered every other window in the house from his room. He had put up thin white curtains in their place, so thin that the sunlight came through during the day and the moonlight at night. When the window was opened, they danced in the breeze, billowing out like the sails of a ship. When Arhen had gone, I begged to move the curtains to my own room, but Aunt Veeva had been firm in refusing. "They are Arhen's curtains," she had said. "He will need them when he comes home."

I straightened the closet and returned all the clothes to their hangers. There were no other signs that I had spent the night in Arhen's room. Reluctant to leave, I sat down in one of the feather-filled chairs and tried to stretch my legs up to the bed as Arhen had always done. Of course, I could not. I am short for a girl, and Arhen was extremely tall.

There is a pair of magic glasses in Arhen's bureau. They magnify everything until you can almost touch it. He used them often to stare out of the window. Since his room is the most perfectly situated, it commands a magnificent view. If you have the mind for such things, you can watch the fields and the creek from his window. The foliage hangs heavy where the fields and river meet, the trees burdened by too much moss and their trunks crowded by underbrush. Girls gather berries there during the warmer months, and men come and bathe naked when the girls have gone. Far upon the hill beyond the river stands the building I am never to mention to Aunt Veeva. It stands cold and austere in the afternoon sun without protection from trees. Although its windows command the same view as Arhen's, I think there are few behind the bars who fancy the scene. I have watched them through the magic glasses, watched them move about inside with their heads lowered.

Arhen says it is wrong to peek at people. He says that people who peek sooner or later see something they do not want to see.

Arhen was right; he always was.

I know that he saw something he did not want to see, something to do with our mother and the doctor who took her away when she died. I remember that day. His face had turned red with anger and the veins on his neck and forehead had swollen until they appeared ready to burst. He had turned the glasses away from the field and had sat on the edge of the bed with his fist clenched and a hissing sound coming from within his throat.

But I had not learned from his lesson.

Not many days ago when aunt Veeva was asleep and the house was quiet, I crept to Arhen's room, took the magic glasses from his bureau, and carried them to his window. When I grew tired of watching the field mice at play and the hawks circling above them in hopes that their prey would become careless and afford them a meal, I turned the glasses on the forbidden building.

Standing against the window, his hands locked around the bars, stood a most frightening man. He was unshaven, his hair unruly and fallen about his forehead. I was positive that while I watched him, he was watching me. His eyes, dark and brooding, were unblinking, wild like those of an animal caught in a trap. It was easy to understand that his thoughts were of freedom; his eyes demanded more of a view than the river afforded him. He longed to bathe in the river, to lie naked on the banks in the afternoon sun, perhaps to run through the fields—to run all the way to Clarke House.

A shiver ran through my body and I pulled the glasses away from my eyes. I returned them to Arhen's bureau, shoving them deep into a stack of his clothes. I knew I would not sleep for many nights remembering the man's face, a familiar yet unknown face, with eyes that would haunt my dreams.

I took a final look about my brother's room.

The girl in the photograph continued to smile although her reason seemed even more distant. I silently informed her that this would be our last meeting. I would not come to Arhen's room again; his room, like Grandfather Clarke's, would remain closed from this day forward.

CHAPTER SIX

Aside from raising chickens and supplying our eggs, Polly who lived in a shack on the river road near the edge of our property, was the only practicing witch I knew who made her occupation public.

She was said to travel to Egypt, Tibet, and even the Amazon River in search of the herbs, grasses, leaves and animals used in the brew that always steamed in the cauldron over the open fire in the middle of her shack. Her shack smelled foul, as did Polly herself. Neither had been cleaned since my first visit. I think this had more to do with her laziness than her busy schedule of astro traveling.

Polly was a thin woman with arms almost absent of flesh and legs that were so brittle it seemed a wonder they managed to support her frame. Her hair was black without the grey of age. Her fingernails were never cleaned and there were grayish scales on her legs and arms.

Polly was respected by the townspeople because she used her witchcraft to cure them of any number of ailments. When first we met it was her wish to have me join her. It was she who gave me the name of Devil Child, claiming she knew by my eyes that I was possessed and could be invaluable in curing the sick.

I declined because I had no wish to aid the townspeople in any manner, even if my apprenticeship would teach me the arts I longed to understand. Polly said she understood my reasoning, but I suspect she blamed my refusal on her inability to bring Arhen home after he had been taken away.

She suspected me also of practicing the black arts on my own. She did not trust me. When in my presence she made sure her lips were tightly sealed so I would not be able to count her teeth, a practice fatal to the victim of a powerful witch; nor would she meet my eyes directly.

On each of my visits I questioned her about the future, but she generally declined an answer, saying all answers would come to me when the timing was right with the stars, not before. Only once did she answer otherwise, and that when I had asked her if Aunt Veeva's power equaled her own.

"We are as different as night and day," she said. "Veeva Clarke belongs to the night."

And of my black periods:

"Excesses," she said. "Mix too much love with too much hate and the soul becomes intoxicated and confused."

As a remedy she suggested I place a can of nails under the eaves to collect the rain and to drink the contents when the rust covered the top.

I decided I would rather have the black periods.

Despite her dislike for his job at the lumber mill and the arguments it created, Arhen had always been Aunt Veeva's favorite. There was a strange bond between them that both pleased and worried me. During the times when all was well between them, there was peace in the house, but the slightest misplaced word in a conversation and the peace would be shattered and replaced by an undercurrent of friction. The last days before Arhen went away it was the friction that prevailed through our days together.

There were moments when I longed for some of the affection Aunt Veeva so lavishly forced on Arhen; but such longings were kept to myself and shall remain buried within me where they cannot be seen. It was right, I thought, that Arhen should receive her love. He was strong and tall and handsome and did not suffer from my affliction of dark moments. He was not possessed as I was. His lack of fear of the outside world was, I think, part of his appeal to Aunt Veeva. She envied him his trips beyond the gates of Clarke House. He was strong in ways where she was weak. He was a great comfort to her, his laughter filling the hollow corners of the house and driving out the lifelessness that lingered during his absences.

With consistency and persistence, Aunt Veeva catered to Arhen's every whim. Her days were spent for the few moments of recognition she would receive from him in the evening when we retired from the dinner table to the library.

Now, looking back on those times before Arhen went away, I can see us huddled in that cluttered room, sullen, waiting to see which way the conversation would begin so that we could adjust to the mood.

Arhen always sat in the big chair behind the desk. It was the largest in the room and suited his frame best. He would stretch his legs out onto the footstool until Aunt Veeva, pretending to be occupied with her needlepoint until she had judged his mood, could finally stand her dejection no longer and would lay aside the material. She would go and push away his feet and seat herself on the stool, and I, Lillith, suddenly the intruder, would curl up beside the fire well removed from the circle of conversation.

Aunt Veeva would always begin by saying his name; slowly, as soft as a summer wind rustling through the willow trees, disjointed, each syllable a name in itself.

"Arh-en." Then she would search her mind for something to draw him out of his quiet and focus his attention on her. "What are the people saying in the town? About us, I mean. Do they still say I was the prettiest girl in the county?"

He would smile, that Arhen smile that was so exclusively his, beginning so secretly about the corners of his mouth and then spreading slowly across his entire face. I would never become fully accustomed to Arhen's smile. It was a many-meaning thing—angels and demons all lurking together about the corners of his mouth, waiting to see which would dominate his expression.

"They still do," he answered. Then assuming the voice of some unknown personage: "That Veeva Clarke is the prettiest girl in the county, in the world. That's what they are saying. Every time they mention . . . your name."

"Do they wonder why I have locked myself away? Do they ask you?"

"Constantly."

"But you don't tell them?"

"Never. I know you wouldn't want that, Veeva dear. I just let them go on talking about how pretty you are, and they go on looking at me sideways as if expecting me to break down at any moment and tell them all the mysteries locked up in Clarke House."

The mysteries of Clarke House?

I would look away from the fire long enough to see if God or the devil had truly worked some magic on Aunt Veeva's appearance. Bent forward, staring from between my arm and chest, I would see the hands the disease had already begun to gnarl and the face that had been mercilessly treated by time, and I would wonder if her beauty had been a truth or a mere fragment of two wistful minds.

"They mustn't ever know, Arhen. They mustn't! You won't get to drinking sometime and tell them, will you?"

"No! Never!" he promised, and I would wonder at the strange expression that crossed his face. Then the smile died on his lips. He leaned forward and lay a hand on her shoulder. I could tell that she shivered beneath his touch. "You really haven't changed all that much," he lied. "You've still got that old *magic*. You're pretty, Veeva. Still pretty. Say it, say *I'm still pretty.*" He was trying again, laying his repeated trap to draw her outside the house, and she was unsuspecting.

"As pretty as your mother?" she begged.

"Prettier," he assured her.

"Mother's dead," I reminded them. It did not seem fair that they should speak of her as they did.

They both looked at me as if realizing for the first time that the girl beside the fire lived and breathed and sponged up their words. But their attention belonged to me for only a second of time before they went back to talking in hushed tones.

Aunt Veeva was caught. "Someday, Arhen! Someday I'll go as far as the road with you, I promise." She had known all along what he wanted. It was written all over his face. She knew he wanted her to leave the house with him. If she had suspected the reason, she would not have been so quick to repay him for his flattery.

"Tomorrow?"

She recoiled, almost slipping from the tool. "No! Not tomorrow! I'm not ready. Not tomorrow, Arhen."

Arhen sighed and sank back in his chair, pretending his disappointment was too much to bear. He shifted his weight and half turned in his seat, as if he wished she would leave him so he could return his feet to the stool and his mind to other matters. She bent forward with the realization of his thoughts as though a pain had suddenly stabbed at her abdomen.

"Must it be tomorrow?" she pleaded.

"No," Arhen told her flatly. "Not tomorrow, or any day. You're afraid. I haven't time for your fears."

"But they might see me. I don't want to be seen, Arhen. Arhen, please forgive me, but I just can't be seen. How can I be seen like this: How can I destroy the only thing I have left? Let them go on talking, Arhen. Let them think I am still beautiful."

"No one will see you," he promised. "The road goes to the mine, the old gold mine. You know it has been closed for years." He leaned forward, thinking he had finally caught her. "You remember the wild cherries beside the road? They're in bloom now. And the brook that runs down from the mountains? It's choked with wild flowers, poppies and larkspur and lily of the valley, all growing so close they make a natural carpet." He watched the memories he stirred reflected on her face. "Don't you want to see that again?"

"I do," she said weakly. "I really do, but—" She was frightened now, knowing he had backed her into a corner and had given her no means of escape. If she refused him, he would turn away from her. They would argue and she did not have the strength tonight. He had drained it from her.

"Will you go with me?" he urged. "Will you go as far as the mine road?"

Her back gave little jerking motions, revealing to me the pain she held inside.

"Maybe," she told him. "Maybe I'll go tomorrow if I'm—"

"Maybe?" He would accept nothing less than an unbreakable promise.

"All right, Arhen! Tomorrow! I'll go tomorrow!" She left the stool and returned to her needlepoint, the promise still hanging in the air between them. Her needle moved in and out of the canvas, in and out, slowly, deliberately painstakingly. Holding the needle firmly, her fingers moved with amazing surety, guiding its way along the line of the flowery pattern.

Please, I prayed, do not let her break down in front of Arhen. Do not let her shed a single tear. He was watching her closely, waiting. He would see the tiniest bit of moisture. His eyes were half-closed, pretending to sleep, but the smile still played about the corners of his mouth, he was still watching.

Her chair faced him directly. She had arranged it that way herself so they might look at each other during our evenings in the library. She had set her own trap.

She fidgeted, pretending occupation with the dull pattern of the needlepoint. The needle moved more rapidly, in and out, in and out, the yarn moving through the canvas loud enough to be heard.

"There's a hole in the roof of my room," I said suddenly. "Someone should fix it before it rains, otherwise everything will get wet."

Silence was my answer. I might as well not have attempted to change the turn of moods.

"I can see light through it at night."

Talk to me, Aunt Veeva. Trust me! I won't say mean things. I won't try to drag you away from the house. Arhen is just bad tonight, in one of his strange moods. You should have been able to tell before you let him corner you. Talk to me. Don't cry.

"Arhen could fix the roof," I persisted. "He can climb on things."

"Perhaps he will, Lillith," she finally said. "He can fix most anything . . . almost."

She rose suddenly, jabbing her needle into a pincushion and dropping the needlepoint onto her chair.

Arhen's eyes ceased to pretend weariness. He pulled himself erect in his chair and casually ran his hand through his dark hair.

"I'll retire now," Aunt Veeva announced. "I'll rest. Goodnight, Arhen. Goodnight, Lilly, dear. Don't forget to close the fire screen."

"Goodnight," Arhen said, quietly. He returned his feet to the footstool and picked up a book from the desk. "See you *tomorrow.*"

"Yes, she stammered. "Tomorrow."

Both Arhen and I knew she would be stricken by one of her attacks during the night. She would not even bother to leave her room tomorrow morning. Even Arhen couldn't expect her to keep her promise when she was ill—not even Arhen.

By tomorrow night she would have regained her fight, the fight that allowed her to argue about his mob at the lumber mill.

Anyway, she would say, *the promise of leaving the house was a mere silliness brought on by my oncoming attack.*

She had no intention of being seen by the townspeople, none at all. What did Arhen mean by coaxing her to abandon her retirement? She had made a solemn oath when her father had leaped through the window of his bedroom that she would never again be seen outside Clarke house. She had repeated that oath the day her sister, our mother, had had her first fatherless child.

The door closed softly behind her as she left the library. I listened until her feet had made the required thirty-two steps to her bedroom before turning to my bother.

"Why do you do that, Arhen?" I asked. "Why do you hate her so much?"

He looked at me as if he had not expected such insight from a young girl.

"You wouldn't understand," he finally said. "I owe it to someone, all that hate." He turned his chair so he faced the darkened window. "You wouldn't understand if I explained it."

"Did you owe the same hate to mother?" I persisted.

He did not answer.

"Aunt Veeva loves you, Arhen. You are her entire world."

"Sometimes," he said without turning, "love can be as destructive as hate. But it isn't love that makes her cling to me." His tone told me I should not pursue the subject.

Arhen turned back to the desk, but reaching for a book, he held it so I could not see his face.

Uneasy suddenly at being left alone with my brother on one of his dark nights, I went back to staring into the fire, wondering if I would ever understand the mysteries of Clarke House of which he had spoken.

CHAPTER SEVEN

I t was early morning.

Dressed only in my nightgown and suffering from the cold, I sat quietly beside Aunt Veeva's bed, summoned from a deep sleep by her cries.

The sun had not yet climbed above the mountain ridges, but its glow already announced the beginning of another day.

Aunt Veeva's darkened form was outlined against the lighter grey of her night shade. "Arhen is mine," she suddenly mumbled. "I claimed him from the beginning. I took him in my arms when he was born and kissed his red little face. *He's mine*, I told her. And she didn't even dispute my claim. She just lay there staring up at me, drained from the labor and delivery.

Old Polly said: 'Don't talk foolishness.' But what did I care what that half-witted creature said?"

I sat on the cot Aunt Veeva allowed me to occupy on rainy nights, aware that I was unimportant to her at times like these, a mere listener to her uncontrolled ramblings.

"Just because a woman gives birth to a child doesn't make her a mother. Motherhood is more than giving birth. Arhen understood. It was his aunt who was his real mother. I was the one he came to with his troubles, with his hurts and questions. Even before she . . . oh, God! It was me he loved, not her."

It was not true, I thought. Arhen didn't love either of them. He only loved me, Lillith Clarke, his sister. Only me. He loved me more than any other person in the world. I remember when I told him that. Didn't he say the same thing to me? *Lillith, I love you more than any other person in the world.* Didn't he?

"Poor fatherless children," Aunt Veeva groaned. "She had no right, no right at all. I was the one who cared, who wanted children. I was the one who cleaned after Arhen and took care of him and saw to his needs. She went on slipping away behind the house, waiting in the woods for the men from the mill. O, God, the disgrace of it! She let them take her on the river bank. A whore, she was no more than a whore! Arhen knew. I saw that he knew. That's why he turned to me. I was his real mother."

Birds were darting about outside. Their shadows blending with Aunt Veeva's silhouette made a strange pattern on the night shade. Soon the sun would be up. Perhaps then she would sleep and I could escape. I knew through past experience that she did not know it was I who sat beside her; she was lost to recognition. I could have been a neighbor—if we had had neighbors who came calling—or a wandering preacher to whom she wished to confide. I knew she had taken some of her medicine. It always affected her in the same manner. Each time I had sat beside her while she talked on and on, forgetting whose ears listened to her ramblings, or lies, or curses, whatever they might be.

"Then her second bastard was born. I often wondered who its father was. Some tramp from the train yards, no doubt. Some mental reject who passed his sickness on to the child. She didn't care. She never considered what disease might be pulsing through a man's veins. She took him the same as the others and had the child with the fits. She'll never be right in the head. Never!"

It took several moments for me to comprehend that I was the child of whom she spoke. The realization seemed to stifle the breath in my lungs. My chest filled with pain and my eyes burned.

"Half-wit!" Aunt Veeva mumbled. "Truly the product of an evil union."

No! I silently protested. *My mother was a beautiful witch and my father was the god of shadows and light. They met in a mist and lay down on green moss to plant the seed of my life.*

"She tells me, 'I love having children.' It was as if it were less than a bitch having pups."

My mother was a witch, I kept repeating to myself. My mother was a witch and my father was the god of shadows and light. They met in a mist and . . . !

"'Just you wait,' I told her. 'Just you wait until they know what you are. Wait until they turn against you.' But I knew she did not take stock in what I said. She paid for her sins. She paid the highest price possible. I saw to that."

. . . planted the seed of my life.

"Arhen will come home. He is not gone for good. Some night he will knock on the door and take me away from Clarke House. We'll walk to where the road meets the path, where the lily of the valley grows so thick, and he'll take my hand in his. 'Mother,' he'll say, 'I missed you so much. You're pretty, mother. You're the prettiest woman in the entire county.' We'll go somewhere to live by the ocean. We'll be able to hear the waves on the shore in the quiet of night, and during the day the horizon will be crowded with sails. Arhen loves me. He had no feeling for my sister, no feeling at all, except maybe shame. Arhen won't blame me for what I did."

Aunt Veeva's hair had fallen free of its pins. It lay over the pillow, glowing silver in the increasing light of morning.

"Father knew what she was like. He knew what shame she brought to his name."

Aunt Veeva's medicine was made of roots. It was I who collected them for her. She had told me exactly how to locate them in the woods, hidden in the shade of the tallest trees. Under her watchful eye, I had crushed them into a pulp and mixed them with water from the tap. Somehow it did not seem right that a medicine should have such effect on the mind. Next time she sent me searching I would collect a different, harmless root, one that Polly might recommend with coaxing.

"Father cursed her. He told her she was unfit to bear a child as perfect as Arhen. 'My little Veeva,' he told her, 'she should have the children, children with a decent father and a name of their own.' Oh, he knew. It was the knowing that drove him to the window. Her sins caused him to fling himself through the glass to the stones below. That's what the shame of her did to him. Those townspeople, what do they know? They say he was possessed, just like his granddaughter. They say he had fits. What do they know?"

Dreamlike, her hand reached out for the glass beside the pitcher, and I, daring to defy her, quickly snatched the glass from her reach.

"It's gone," I told her. "There isn't anymore."

She turned and stared at me through the morning greyness, bringing her hand to her eyes to ward off the approaching glare of the light. "No more? Arhen? Is that you?"

"It's Lillith," I told her, apologetically. "You drank all the medicine. Should I get you some water?"

"Water?" she said weakly. "Yes, please, Lilly. I am thirsty. I need cold water."

I carried the pitcher into the bathroom and emptied the remainder of the medicine into the bowl. After rinsing it thoroughly, I filled it with water and returned to her room.

She had turned on her side, and had raised the shade higher to watch the birds darting about among the tangle of vines.

"Do you know that my father has a picture of me in his room, Lilly? It was one of his favorite possessions, taken the day of my nineteenth birthday. I'm dressed all in pink—pink dress and hat with a long pink ribbon. You can't tell from the picture, of course, since it's black and white, but I remember the lovely pink of that dress. It was a present from father, and the picnic was a special treat. We were always allowed one wish for our birthdays. My wish was that we could go on a picnic without Echo." She laughed softly, "How that upset her. But he granted me my wish."

The sun was now above the mountain ridges. The room was filled with the intense light; the shadows were gone from the corners, and Aunt Veeva, bathed in the light, seemed more herself than she had in the darkness. She turned and looked at me, blinking.

"Your water," I said, setting the pitcher on the table beside her bed. I poured her a glassful and, attempting to raise her head with my hand, put the glass to her lips.

"I'm not entirely helpless," she said. She took the glass from me. "It's morning already." She drank sparingly and returned the glass to the table. "I'm so tired. It was a bad night—the worst in a long while."

"It's the weather," I told her. "You always have bad nights when the weather changes."

"Yes. That must be it. The weather is so unpredictable during this time of year."

"Do you want breakfast now?"

"No. I think I will sleep more. Leave me be until I call you." She pulled the blankets up about her chin. "You know, I must have been dreaming of Arhen last night. He is so strongly on my mind."

As I left the room, she reached up and pulled down the night shade, covering herself in darkness.

"Sleep well," I whispered.

She moaned softly in reply.

Outside of her room, I stood with my back against the door. "Arhen," I whispered, "what have you done? What have you done to Aunt Veeva?"

But I could not fairly blame Arhen for something I did not understand, so I blamed the house. Although it was crumbling, it was strong enough to bear the burden.

Somewhere in Clarke House, where I hid it and do not remember where, is a book of Arhen's drawings. They are bound by a blood red binding and a wine-colored string holds the seams together, those white pages so defiled by his charcoal pencils. I found the book in the lower drawer of the desk and decided it should be hidden more secretly.

Across the front page in large slanting letters he had written his name—ARHEN CLARKE—and after his name, he has scrawled the word PRIVATE. Behind that name page, hiding under the word PRIVATE, is the first drawing: the building which stands on the cliff with the foreground an exaggeration of the river scene from his window, the parasitic moss and mistletoe hanging from the trees as if they were in complete possession of their host. The building itself rises before the morning sun, a tabernacle, outlined by waving lines representing the rays of the rising sun which it blocks.

The second drawing is an orange and black sketch of a frail person that must surely be me. I am standing in the garden below his window, my hands outstretched and used as a perch by a large vulturous bird; the other hand is raised to protect my eyes from its beak.

The third drawing is of a woman, grotesquely mutilated by his art. Her body is twisted and her hands clutch at her throat as if she is having great difficulty breathing. The same bird lurks in the background of this sketch . . . watching and waiting for the woman's final gasps of life.

Somewhere in Clarke House, where I hid it and try not to remember where, is a book of Arhen's drawings. They are not for other eyes, those drawings, and the word PRIVATE seems too weak a warning to any who might open the cover.

Monday is the loneliest day of the week. At seven-thirty the mill whistle breaks the silence, announcing that beyond the walls of our house there is a life cycle beginning anew. Men are making lumber for houses and paper for books as Arhen had done. Some man is leaping about the millpond in his place, dragging logs toward the big chain that will carry them to the jaws of the saws. The metal cones are fed new life, and spiral their black smoke high into the sky above the valley. In their kitchens, women are getting their children off to school and thinking of the noonday meal.

I also have a cycle that begins each Monday.

I begin the day by gathering the tools from the shed and carrying them into the back garden away from Aunt Veeva's prying. I plunge the spade into the ground and turn the earth over on the surface, black and rich with life. Into the holes I place things I have collected during the week: leaves from the oak tree, a broken twig from the lilac bush, a label from a can of tomatoes, anything worth burying that my eyes have fallen upon. Once I planted seeds from an orange and a fresh plum, but nothing ever grew. Now I plant only things that have been forgotten, useless things that would be best under the ground. Then I push the dirt back over the intruding rubbish with my hands and pack it tight with the hoe. If the wind is not blowing in the direction of Aunt Veeva's window and she cannot possibly hear me, I repeat a canticle from one of the books on witchcraft taken from her bedside table.

I love the smell of the earth. I love the feel of its richness against my skin, and the knowledge that there is no richer earth anywhere in the valley than behind the walls of Clarke House.

There was a time when the gardens were a jungle of plants. Flowers bloomed in all the planters and shrubs lined every wall, forming a path from the back of the house to the front gate. The trellis leaned under a burden of bougainvilleas, threatening to collapse—as it later did—and bury the walkways under hard-to-clear vines. The statues were not hidden within tangles of briars as they now stand, with only a marble hand or foot exposed, beckoning, pleading for the sun.

That time was before the witch grass blew over the wall and took possession—before mother dies and Arhen went away. That time is but a fading memory kept alive with more difficulty each day.

Someday I will make the gardens beautiful again. I will burn out all the strangling weeds and plant only wild and beautiful things, larkspur and poppies and dandelions. I'll rebuild the gazebo, and on hot nights I will sleep there away from the mocking darkness of the house.

CHAPTER EIGHT

The furthest point to which I have ventured from Clarke House is the wooden bridge that crosses Rueben Creek.

Since the bridge is in the direction of the town, I would never have been so brave if the heavy undergrowth lining the banks did not make a thick, concealing cover. I knew no villager would tear his way through the dense entanglement and discover me lurking there. The scratches they would earn for their effort were not worth the fun of tormenting a young girl. Even the animals that lived along the creek's banks were safe from trappers, living peacefully in their world of briars and thistles. The creek ran within a few feet of the walls of Clarke House, another reason I considered the bridge safe ground. It would be an easy matter to slip quickly through the gate and escape capture should the need arise.

The bridge is my second private place, second only to the lean-to in the woods, because Arhen did not build it but I had claimed possession because of my ability to reach its underside without detection. Once beneath, I would sit on the only dry area, a raised knoll, where I had my choice of two views. To the left, the creek ran back toward Clarke House in its haste to join the river; to the right, if you held firmly to the bottom of the timbers and leaned out over the water, you could see the edge of the town itself, the great white steeple of the church rising above the trees. Sometimes I saw some of the hateful town youths lolling about the dock near the bend, trying without success to skip rocks across the white current.

There were only a few men who used the path and Rueben Creek bridge. These were the mill hands who lived in the quarry and had to make their way to the footbridge to reach their jobs at the mill. They passed in the morning and again at night. Those that did travel this route always seemed to stop on the bridge. The bridge was the halfway point between the quarry and the lumber mill, but I think it was the view of Clarke House that caused them to pause. Of course, none of the passersby realized that beneath the boards at their feet, watching them through the cracks, hid a troll named Lillith

Clarke, a coward too frightened to protect her bridge and order them to be on their way.

On Tuesday, I had hardly reached the safety of the bridge when I heard two men approaching along the path. I crouched back against the bridge frame, afraid they had seen me as I had dashed for safety. If they had, they would peer through the cracks in the boards; they would point and laugh and call names, and the bridge would be lost to me from that time on.

They moved onto the bridge and came to a halt. I could tell by the amount of light the soles of their shoes hid over the cracks that they were grown men, not boys hiding from school. One of them wore a green and white striped jacket, and the other had spikes on the bottom of his boots. I knew he was a pond man. He must have taken Arhen's job guiding the logs. The man in the green and white striped jacket was smaller in size. Moving forward until he stood at the end of the bridge, he removed a package of cigarettes from his pocket and offered one to his companion.

The pond man accepted. He struck a match to the ends of each of their cigarettes, inhaled deeply, and tossed the match over the edge of the bridge. It was quickly caught up by the current and carried away. Then the man leaned heavily on one leg. His spikes dug into the wood, tearing away splinters along the edges of the cracks.

"If that damned Clarke House were tore down a man wouldn't have to walk three extra miles to the mill," he said, bitterly.

His companion grunted in agreement, walked to the edge of the platform, and spit tobacco juice into the water. "It's the walls that get me," he said. "There's enough concrete in that wall to stretch from here to Hugo and back again. And what's the good? I don't think the walls make a damned bit of difference. There's not many who'd want to get inside."

"Could be they're afraid of getting out," the pond man said with a chuckle.

"They say the Devil Child goes wild in the woods back there behind the house. I heard she says prayers to Satan himself."

"Yeah, I heard that," the pond man announced. "I heard she strips naked and dances along the river bank, singing and crying." A moment of silence passed. "How old she suppose to be now? In her early teens, isn't she?"

"It's her mind that didn't grow. She's possessed, just like her grandfather. Devil's fits, that's what they had." He dropped his cigarette into the water and squatted on one knee, staring off toward the house. "I heard old man Thomas used to meet her by the river on Sundays." He spit again and the black liquid settled in the fork of cattail stalks.

"I don't believe that," the pond man announced. "I was sort of fond of that old guy. I'll admit he was the strangest man alive outside those walls at Clarke House and that loony pen on the hill."

Another silence followed. Then the little man spoke again: "Too bad about him. He was all right. He used to hang around the mill a lot asking if we needed a good man. Then he brought the Clarke kid in."

Mr. Thomas! What are they saying? Why do they speak of you in such tones? Have you gone to Hugo for the final time without even saying goodbye? Won't we have another Sunday by the river, one more Sunday of meeting and talking and being friends? Oh, Mr. Thomas! I was going to ask you to live in Clarke House. You could have had my old room. I cleaned it. I washed away the cobwebs and made the bed with fresh linen. It's waiting for you—and you've already gone to Hugo.

"They say he made a pillow out of leaves," the pond man said.

"I saw it. Most weird thing I ever did see. There it was, a nice little stack of leaves all pushed up in a pile with blood all over them."

"Must have done it because he was so old."

"Or sick, or something. His daughter Kathryn said she just couldn't understand it. She said he seemed happy enough Monday morning. They were planning a trip to Hugo on the following Sunday. He talked about it all during breakfast. After he ate, she said he just got up, kissed her goodbye, and walked out of the house without saying a word. When he didn't come home by dark, she called out the volunteers. We found him down by the river near the footbridge."

"It was his son-in-law's gun, wasn't it?"

"So they tell me. They say he took it without them noticing. Only took one bullet. I guess he knew it wouldn't take more than that."

"People do funny things for funny reasons," the pond man mumbled. "When you know you're going to put a bullet through your head, why make a pillow of leaves like you wanted to be all comfortable like?"

"Beats me."

"You going to the funeral tomorrow?"

"No. I can't stand that sort of thing. Gives me the creeps seeing people carrying on over a dead person, especially women. They hate a person all their life, then when that person dies they weep like it was a close relation." He grunted. "Of course, his daughter is pretty broken up. She's a real nice girl. Married that Andrade boy last year."

The pond man threw his cigarette into the water and started on across the bridge, his companion close at his heels. Their footsteps left the wooden planks and their voices began to die in the dust of the path.

"If they would tear down that damned Clarke House a man wouldn't have to walk three extra miles to the mill every day."

"Maybe they will someday. It can't stand like that for much longer. It's the walls that get me. Why would Jake Clarke go and put up a . . ."

Clutching my chest, I ran for the underbrush before I screamed. Then falling on my back and staring up through the arch of trees and briars, the demon inside of me broke free. My screams must have cut through the quiet of the morning more shrilly than the mill whistle. They must have been heard across the fields, even in the heart of the town, but they did not reach within the blackness that claimed me.

Aunt Veeva was trying not to smile at the news I brought her about Mr. Thomas' suicide. Her long grudge against him had been nursed too long for her not to enjoy a moment of victory. She wanted to laugh. She wanted to laugh as she did when I told her about the boy who fell in the mud. Her lips ached to smile with amusement. She will, I thought, deny me the right to grieve.

Closing the Bible which lay on her lap when I entered, she pushed it under her pillow. She folded her hands and looked at me, waiting for me to speak the words I kept trying to force between my teeth.

I stood stuttering for several moments, feeling my face flush and my hands tremble. A short scene flashed before my eyes of Arhen and Aunt Veeva in the library with him trying to coax her beyond the walls into the outside world. I felt her struggle as if it were my own.

"To . . . tomorrow . . . I . . ."

"Come out with it, Lillith!" Aunt Veeva demanded. She pulled herself up impatiently against her pillows. "Say what you want to say. Then leave me. I want to be alone." The smile returned to her lips. "I want to lie here and think of that old fool killing himself."

My hands suddenly ceased trembling. Something inside my head seemed to snap and the sound echoed through my head as I heard myself saying: "Tomorrow I am going to his funeral!"

There was laughter then. Its amused cruelty sent me running from the room, my hands clamped about my ears.

CHAPTER NINE

Clarke County is extremely small, but my knowledge of it is smaller still, limited to the property line of Clarke House, the woods, the bridge, and through listening to Arhen and Mr. Thomas, vaguely to the village itself. I know that to reach the town from the north you have to travel to the main road, turn right and cut back at the base of the mountain. Or, if you are inclined and at home among the trees and underbrush, you can cut through the area called The Jungle by the young people and come out in the lumber yard not more than a quarter of a mile from the whitewashed church.

If there was a death in the valley, the mill generally closed in respect to the deceased. There would be no men climbing around on the stacks of freshly cut wood, no curious eyes peeking out from inside the guard house, none of the hateful women waiting around for their men to stop for lunch—no one to see who came out of The Jungle.

I came to the edge of the undergrowth and stood looking out over the stacks of lumber. It was a grey, overcast day; the sun had risen early and then retired behind threatening clouds. A semi-darkness was cast over the yards, giving the lumber the appearance of something deserted long ago and left to rot without need. There were no men in sight, no caretaker in the little shack near the center of the yard. A dog lazed in the weeds near the ditch, rolling his eyes toward me, disinterested, it seemed, with my concern. I glared back at him as if he, being a possession of a hateful one, also questioned my right to trespass.

The church steeple rose beyond the yard. Between the stacks of lumber, I could see an occasional black-bedecked villager move along the path toward the church door. The bell tolled slowly, either in respect for my friend or because the arm of the toller had grown weary. Each ring echoed off the hills and came back to meet its predecessor in a duel of tonelessness.

I had found a dress which had belonged to my mother. It was dark blue, but in the darkness of the church I expected it to appear black. The skirt was long and there was an excess of fabric about the bodice. Aside from the dress, found in a trunk in the basement, everything else belonged to me and was inappropriate; my coat, red and white plaid, would have to be discarded immediately inside the church door, and I would be forced to sit with my feet pulled back well under the bench to hide the fact that I wore sneakers dyed black. Already the damp earth in the woods had caused the dye about the soles to run and the white was showing through.

Now, peering out from the edge of the undergrowth, I appraised my clothes and felt a sense of shame. I knew I looked demented. It would take more than mother's dress to hide my tomboyishness. What would the townspeople say when they saw me enter the church? Perhaps they would drag me to the door and deny me entrance.

When the flow of hateful ones entering the church had stopped, I came out from the protection of the woods and moved toward the church, determined that I should pay my final respects to Mr. Thomas. After all, wasn't it what he had wanted most? My coming away from Clarke House? This one time, just this one time, I intended to be seen and not to run for the safety of the woods. Only that could repay him for the kindness he had shown me on Sundays. I would not look at his daughter, but I would mark the feeling of her presence for that time when I could deliver her destruction in an explosion of witchcraft. I would feel, and I would see through my mind's eye that creature who drove my friend to his end.

My steps were slow, my mind set on reaching the church without thinking of the strangeness of my being where I was. The bell had stopped tolling and had left an ominous silence behind.

"Hey, half-wit!"

The suddenness of the voice butting through the silence caught me unaware. I must have screamed my fright for it seemed to echo like the last tolling of the bell.

"It's the crazy Clarke girl! I'll be damned! Will you look at her!" The youth giggled, and I spun around to face him.

There were four of them, all young, dressed in bleached coveralls and wearing red hunting hats on the backs of their heads. When I had spun around at the sound of their voices they had started forward, but one, he who towered above the others in size and ugliness, held up his hand, and his companions came to a halt like a patrol of perfectly trained soldiers.

"You know what they say," he said, "about this one being some kind of devil creature—a witch. You don't just walk up to a witch. It's not polite." He smiled, his lips curling away from chipped front teeth. "She's not half as ugly as they say." He took one step forward and I stepped back. "She may put a curse on us," He said with a laugh. "Or maybe she'll go into one of those devil fits."

"I bet she don't have no blood in her," said the boy nearest my own size. I instinctively hated him more than the others. His evilness oozed from his eyes. "That's why she's a half-wit. She don't have any blood to feed her brain."

"Maybe she's a killer like her big brother," suggested another.

"I still bet she don't have any blood in her. Look how white she is. That's not natural."

I backed against the lumber stack and felt the splinters dig into my coat. *Arhen*, I thought, *they've got me now—just like they got you.* I looked around for the quickest exit to the woods, but the stacks of lumber were like a maze, hiding everything from view except the church at one end and The Jungle at the other. The boys blocked the undergrowth. There was only the church open to me.

The dog that had been lying beside the ditch rose and came slowly forward as if someone had finally invented a game worthy of his attention. He stopped beside the boys and stood watching me through lowered eyes, his tail wagging slowly and his head lowered like a wild boar ready to attack.

"Coming to the funeral, half-wit?"

The fourth member of the group had stepped aside, and was leaning against the opposite end of the stack of lumber that supported my weight. We stood like two engaged in a game of tag, the stack of lumber being "safe base." If I didn't move, I would be safe. If I didn't move, they could not touch me.

"Old man Thomas blew out what brains he had," the leader announced. "Or at least that's what my old lady told me."

"Yeah, they're not goin' to open the casket. Can't look at a man with no brains left in his head."

They advanced a couple of steps as if some silent signal had been given by their leader. The one my size removed his hat and flung it on the ground where they watched the dog examine it as a curiosity. The others followed his example. The boy at the end of "Safe base" began to roll up his shirt sleeves.

"Let's see if she has any blood in her."

"No, don't go getting rough, Jake," the leader said. He stared at me through slits in his eyelids. "We don't want to hurt the pretty girl. We just want to look at her—all over—and see what makes her different than other girls."

He's the ugliest, I thought. That's why he was their leader. I brought the material of Mama's dress together about my throat, digging my nails into my own flesh.

"We'll do to her what they say Arhen did to my sister."

His sister? I suddenly visualized the girl in the photograph in Arhen's room. Could this grotesque creature be her brother? And Arhen—what had he done to her?

"Arhen," I repeated like a dumb thing. "Arhen."

"Yes, Arhen," the leader hissed. "I saw him the night he killed the doctor. Your whore Mama's lover."

"Arhen never killed nobody!" I screamed.

"Sure he did. You think they came and took him away because he was so pure?"

"Arhen just went away! He's coming home. Aunt Veeva says he'll come home any day now!" Maybe, I thought, the idea of facing my bother would hold them at bay.

"Arhen boy coming home!" the boy named Jake laughed. "Arhen's not coming home for a long, long time. They've locked him up good and tight and thrown away the key."

"Yeah, that's what they do to you when you go loony and kill people."

Hateful ones! Lies! All lies!

I'll bet if we cut her, she won't bleed. She don't have no blood to feed her brain. That's why they call her the Devil Child.

"We're not going to cut her," the leader told Jake. "That's not polite. You know what everyone says about the Clarkes. Why, they're the most polite personages in Clarke County. That's why the whole damned place is named after them.

They're so polite and so-o-o crazy! You just don't go and cut a Clarke. Besides, if they had blood it would be blue, real blue."

"What are we going to do with her?" Jake demanded.

The leader scratched his head, trying to look as if he were puzzling an important problem. I bet he has lice, I thought. I hope they suddenly begin biting him and don't stop until there's nothing left but bone. "I thought maybe we'd play a little game," he finally told his companions.

"What kind of game?"

"Like hounds and fox, maybe."

Hounds and fox, I thought. Arhen had never mentioned such a game. He had never tried to teach it to me as he had the other games. What are they going to do to me? If Arhen had hidden it from me, it must have been evil.

"You don't mind playing a little game with us, do you, half-wit? I'll bet you'd enjoy doing something besides hide in that ugly old house with nobody to talk to except your crazy old aunt."

I pulled myself away from the lumber and felt the splinters try to hold my clothing. "I've . . . I've got to go," I mumbled. "I've got to go for Mr. Thomas." I started to move away toward the church, taking steps backward, afraid to let them out of my sight.

The boy leaning against "safe base" stepped forward a couple of steps. Then, suddenly leaping forward, pushed me back against the lumber stack. "You don't want to run off like that," he said. "It's not polite. You heard Georgie. He says you Clarkes are supposed to be polite personages." He was close enough for me to smell his breath.

Georgie came closer, close enough so that I could see the pimples on his cheeks and the stains that darkened his teeth, stains, I knew, which came from the wild tobacco plant. I quickly counted his teeth, knowing each would reduce the span of his life. But George apparently had a long life ahead of him, for although I counted to fifteen, he continued to stand undaunted by the reduction of time. "This little game is simple," he said. "Even a half-wit can understand it. We just take your clothes away. We give you about three minutes head start and then we come looking for you."

"Mama's dress," I bellowed.

"We won't hurt it none. Will we, boys? It's just that a fox don't run around with a nice blue dress on. Besides, taking your clothes away is gonna make it easier for the one who captures you. He gets to find out what makes you so different than other girls."

They had formed a semicircle around me with the lumber blocking my escape from behind. They still kept a light distance, however, waiting for a signal from their leader to tighten the circle and start grabbing at my clothes. Jake, the one I hated most, seemed more anxious that the others. He kept a few inches ahead so that he would be first to spring when the signal was given.

Aunt Veeva! Why didn't you teach me? Why? I closed my eyes and wished on every book I could remember that some portion of the black crafts would become suddenly known to me. I called on every curse. Let them die! Let them die!

Then they struck.

Hands grabbed at my coat. As it was pulled away, my body spun like a top, stopping only after my head smashed against the piling. Pain! My body was filled with nothing but pain! Even my fright seemed to vanish before the pain.

"Make them die!" I screamed.

There was a laugh, a horrible, mocking laugh that went on and on without stopping. Something scratched my face, and a fist found the sensitive area of my abdomen. Instinctively, trapped like one of the wild animals in the woods, I clasped both my hands together and swung forward with all the force within my body. I felt contact. There was the sound of breaking bone. Then all became silent. The hands ceased to pull at my clothes.

I opened my eyes and stared down at Jake, who lay on the ground at my feet. Lying limply with one hand bent beneath him and his head thrown back and resting on a clump of weeds, he resembled a cast-off rag doll; except that he was bleeding, great gushes of bright red blood coming from his nose and running down his cheeks.

His companions bent over, more in amazement than with the intent of helping.

Run, Lillith! Run!

I imagined it was Arhen's voice instructing me.

Jumping past the stooped bodies and overturning the leader, who toppled on top of his unconscious companion, I ran.

"Don't let her get away. We'll get her for this!"

"Can we cut her for Jake?"

"We'll cut her throat!"

I knew I could not reach the woods. Even if I had not become hopelessly confused in my directions, I doubted my strength to run for any distance. My only escape was to hide—hide—hide.

The stacks of lumber had been placed on logs to keep them off the ground. Without stopping to consider the narrow space, I dropped to my stomach and squeezed myself underneath. I lay waiting. From my hiding place I could see the boys' feet, the dirty shoes scrambling this way and then that, pointing, searching. The dog, thinking this was the high point of the game, ran after one and then the other, barking and nipping at their legs.

"Half-wit! Come out, half-wit!"

"Here, little fox."

See Mr. Thomas? See what you wanted to bring me out of Clarke House to face? See why I was afraid?

"Your Aunt Veeva is calling you, half-wit."

"Don't you hear her?"

"She's waiting for you."

"She wants to push you out of the window after her old man."

"Come out, half-wit. Your Aunt Veeva wants to teach you to fly like a bird."

My face was resting on one hand. There was a bruise, red, the skin scraped away. Blood! The knuckles were cut. The skin had been cleanly broken away directly across the knuckles. It must have been from hitting the boy Jake in my desperation to escape. I was actually bleeding!

"Here, Devil girl. Georgie wants to see what makes you different than other girls."

Don't cry, Lillith. Don't cry, or they'll find you. They'll tear Mama's dress off your back and do things to your body, things like you saw in the woods near the swimming hole.

Two feet ran up to the edge of the opening. They turned right and then left. There were metal plates on the toes and heels, metal plates that shone like eyes, cold, but not revealing.

The upper parts of the shoes were worn thin, the leather cracked and uncared for.

"When we find her, I'll bet she don't have no blood in her."

I have!

The feet hurried away.

Then the breath caught in my throat. The blood was forgotten, so was the pain and the fright of the boys. The dust on the ground beyond my hiding place was being spotted by small, deadly drops. Rain! It was going to rain! And I was trapped. If I could make the woods—if I could crawl into the small cave—if I had only not left Clarke House! The hand with the blood dug into the dirt and attempted to pull my body free of my hiding place. It would only be a few minutes. Then the rain would begin. The few scattered drops were only a warning. There would be a few precious moments to spare. Pull! Hurry! You can make it to the woods. There is an old cave just inside The Jungle. Pull! Hurry! Crawl! Use your knees! Hurry, Lillith!

I attempted to wedge my body against the lumber and push forward toward the opening, but in my haste my head shot upward. It struck the bottom of the piling and there was a blackness, an abyss filled with voices, calling:

"Half-wit! Come out!"

We want to watch! We know you're a witch and WE WANT TO WATCH YOU MELT IN THE RAIN!

God in Heaven, or Satan below—one of you spare me!

My hand had developed a personality of its own. It was living suspended from my body, a separate being occupied only by the pain of its cut knuckles. The fingers had dug a small hole in the loose earth beneath the lumber pile, and the hand lay inside as if waiting for the dirt to be pushed over it. The rain water had found the hole and had covered all except the top of the hand, leaving the knuckles exposed above the surface, the cut bleeding still and the blood mingling with the wood pitch and the bits of sawdust.

The voices were gone. Only the sound of the rain remained, not frightening now.

There is nothing to be afraid of, I thought with wonder. The ground beneath you is wet. The rain has found you and you are lying in slime. The coldness beneath your face is rain. Your hand lies in a puddle of rain. Rain! And you have not melted!

My head ached and my vision, attempting to focus on the rain striking the ground beyond the piling, was blurred. The drops struck hard, rose again with the force, and fell back to settle into small streams. It was raining hard, harder than I had ever seen.

I willed my hand to lift itself from the hole and it attached itself once again to the whole of me. The pain shot up my arm and into my head. Pulling myself from under the lumber, I lay face up on the ground, letting the raindrops sting my face. My mouth was open and the coolness trickled down into my throat to quench the burning.

Lillith Clarke, you are not a witch!

I did not mistake the silent voice within my mind for Arhen—or anyone other than myself.

You are not a witch! You are merely a girl who lives in Clarke House—a girl who watches people from behind curtains—a girl who suffers from fits of blackness and bad memory.

"It's true," I said aloud.

No matter what Aunt Veeva tells you, you do not belong to the world of demons and witches, spells and curses. You are—you are a half-wit! There! I've thought it!

"Mama's dress!" I brought my body upright despite the pain in my head and stared down at my mother's dress. It was covered with mud and there was a tear across the bodice where the boys had tried to rip it from me. "Mama, forgive me!" I groaned, but my voice was lost in a howl of the wind.

There was movement at the end of the lumber yard. A procession of umbrella-covered townspeople was moving past the opening between the stacks of lumber. Behind them, moving slowly, came six men carrying a long box. The wreath of flowers that lay on the top was caught by the wind and slipped unnoticed to the muddy ground. After the box had passed, I continued to stare at the wreath. It was not made of wild flowers as it should have been, but of giant foreign blossoms that looked artificial in their perfection. There was the sound of motors starting, then fading as the cars moved away from the front of the church.

"I tried, Mr. Thomas, I tried," I said, and getting to my feet, I stumbled back toward the woods.

The back gate of Clarke House was swinging in the wind. The giant frame struck the wall and sprang forward against its hinges as if it were fighting to be torn free. I slipped inside and slid the heavy bolt into place.

The house was dark except for the light that came from Aunt Veeva's room. She had managed to light the kerosene lantern and had not lowered her night shade. I could see her shadow against the window. One hand was to her eyes, and she stared out into the darkness of the storm. The light behind her outlined her silver hair and the thinness of her arm.

I still wore Mama's dress, not having stopped at the cave to change back into my own clothes. It would not do to have Aunt Veeva see me before I changed. She had an obsession with people's possessions being private. She would be angry beyond words at the mud stains and the unmendable tear.

Stepping back into the shadows of the gate, I stood waiting for a chance to enter the house unseen.

At that moment, as I crouched beside the wall, the sky was streaked with lightning and I was bathed in an intense, momentary light.

Aunt Veeva brought both hands to her face. She pressed herself against the windowpane. Above the wind, the rain, and the thunder, I could hear her scream.

CHAPTER TEN

"Forgive me!" I begged. "Forgive me!"

Aunt Veeva was speechless, staring at me coldly. Her hair had come loose from its combs and lay spread over the satin pillows. Her forehead was streaked with perspiration. Her eyes held an expression foreign to her, an expression easily recognizable as fear. Her voice, also, had been filled with fear when she had thought the figure she had seen in the garden had been someone other than myself.

She shook herself, and her expression changed to anger. "Half-wit!" she snapped.

My head slumped further into the protection of my shoulders. I was waiting for the attack I knew would come.

The wetness of my clothes had suddenly seemed to penetrate my flesh, and the cut on my hand, although the bleeding had stopped, continued to throb with regular stabs of pain. I moved my hand behind my back so Aunt Veeva would not see it.

"What are you hiding?" she demanded, her voice shrill, accusing.

Reluctantly, but hoping for a show of sympathy, I held out my hand and exposed the cut and bruises.

Her expression did not alter. "'I am going to his funeral,'" she mocked. "Well, how does it feel to have been to a funeral?" She waved my hand from her sight. "How does it feel to be beaten and cursed and rejected for your efforts?" She glared at me, waiting for a reply.

"Forgive me," I said again; and could think of nothing else to add.

"Forgive," she echoed. "You've defied me! And what's worse—you've probably brought the wrath of those ignorant villagers upon us again! I can hear them now," she groaned. "All talking in their dirty little peasant houses. 'Better see to the night latch and keep a light burning. Those Clarkes are at it again!' Forgive you? What if they come again? Remember the last time? It will all be your doing if they come!" She clasped her hands together and began to wring them nervously.

My head reeled with her words.

"They're—they're afraid," I mumbled. "Afraid of the house."

"Are they? Were they afraid last time?"

Last time! Last time they had come for Arhen.

That night we had just finished dinner and had gone into the library when the first shouts had torn through the walls and cornered us where we were sitting.

Arhen had suddenly appeared trapped, stunned by their cries. I felt afterward that he had been expecting them, had known they would come but not exactly when, or so soon. They had forced the front door when no one had gone to answer. They had pushed into the library and had stood staring at us sitting in our chairs unmoving.

"We've come for you, Arhen," they had said. "You know why."

Aunt Veeva had screamed. She had thrown her needlepoint canvas onto the floor and had leaped to her feet, running forward with a long needle raised above her head. Before they could stop her, she had stabbed two of the men. Then they had grabbed her arms and twisted her to the floor where she lay sobbing, still searching for the needle that had fallen from her hands in the struggle.

Arhen had sprung out of his chair and pushed me toward the door. "Hide, Lillith," he had cried, but I had huddled against the door frame, too frightened for my legs to carry me from the room.

The villagers had been like wild beasts, moving into the library and circling around Arhen until he was trapped in the center of their numbers. They had closed in slowly around him, waiting, hoping, I thought, for him to attempt to break for freedom. Instead, he had stood quietly, not moving, waiting for them to take him as if he knew struggling would be useless.

"I'm innocent," he had told them. "You're taking an innocent man."

Whatever had been done, the men had not held him blameless. They had carried him away, and Aunt Veeva and I had been left alone on the floor of the library; she holding the needle she had finally recovered, still sobbing and striking at the air, and me, stunned, unable to comprehend that this scene had been a part of reality and not the extension of a nightmare.

Later she told me that it had all been a simple misunderstanding. She had told me that the villagers had set Arhen free and he had gone away because he did not feel he could continue to live among them. He had gone, she had told me, to live near the sea where he would work and save his money and someday come home to Clarke House to take us away.

"Will they come again?" I asked.

Aunt Veeva looked at me, her eyes glazed by thought. Perhaps she, too, was remembering that dreadful night.

Remembering her attack with the needle, the red stains which had streaked one man's face after the plunge of her weapon. Perhaps she was remembering Arhen's submissiveness, the quiet which had settled over the house when he had gone. If they did come again, was she thinking that she would be of no physical aid?

"Will they come again?" I repeated.

"Perhaps not," she finally said. "If we stay away from funerals. Stay where we belong in Clarke House and wait for Arhen to return."

I felt extremely warm. My forehead was burning. The dizziness would not leave me, and I swayed noticeably on my feet.

"What is it?" Aunt Veeva demanded. "What's wrong with you?"

"My head," I mumbled.

Her eyes then showed concern. "Get those wet things off," she instructed. "Dry yourself and go to bed. We can't have you taking another of those attacks."

I looked longingly at the cot beside her bed, but she said nothing, so I went into my own room and closed the door. I stripped off Mama's tattered dress and dried myself. All of my skin seemed to ache, to be screaming with pain under the towel. I wrapped a cloth about the bandage on my hand and crawled weakly into bed.

When sleep came, it was a half-sleep robbed of rest. The scene stamped on the insides of my eyelids would not leave me. I saw Arhen being dragged away. I saw the faces of the boys in the lumberyard fuse with those of the townspeople who had stormed the house. I heard voices calling: *Your Aunt Veeva wants you! She wants to teach you to fly like a bird!*

I saw Mr. Thomas lie down on the ground, his head resting on a pillow of leaves. He put a pistol to his head and gently squeezed the trigger, but when the explosion came it was my head that received the bullet. As the pain shattered inside of me the demon who had been at the front door during the storm suddenly appeared on the edge of the clearing. She dashed forward and gathered up the blood-soaked leaves, running on as she scattered them to the wind.

CHAPTER ELEVEN

The following morning I kept to my bed with a fever, rising only to bring Aunt Veeva her morning coffee and toast. The warm, heavy weight of my blankets gave me a feeling of security, and I slept periodically without dreams.

The storm had not passed, but was resting, gathering strength for a renewed assault. The old, blue panes of the window shone grey, dull, and were frequently set to rattling by the wind.

Waking after a fitful nap, I blamed the wind for having brought me to awareness. Then, muffled by the closed door, I heard voices from Aunt Veeva's adjoining room. Slipping from bed, I crossed my room and crouched beside the keyhole.

"My father often spoke of your niece," a soft voice said. "His last few days were spent talking of little else. He seemed deeply concerned about the girl's welfare."

"Indeed?" Aunt Veeva's voice was sharp, bitter.

"You can certainly understand that concern," the voice persisted. "Only the child and you living here in this big house, and—and you crippled. There are many of us who have concerned ourselves with your problem—with . . ."

". . . with what should be done with us," Aunt Veeva finished. "I know these villagers. I knew your father. We were children together. He was always pompous, always sticking his nose in where it was not his concern. He delighted in other people's affairs."

"Miss Clarke! Please! My father is dead! Surely he deserves the respect afforded the departed."

"Departed!" Aunt Veeva sneered. "Respect is not earned by six feet of topsoil."

"Neither is it earned by shutting one's self away from the outside world," the voice snapped, "nor by burying a defenseless child with you in your private hell."

"Enough! You had best sneak out as you sneaked in," Aunt Veeva cried. "Your father was not welcome here. And there is no welcome for you. We, my niece and I, have chosen to bury ourselves from the outside world. The child is contented here with me. What is there outside for her? She's ill. She needs me."

"I believe it is you who need her," the visitor dared. "My father believed the same. He said you filled the child with fantasies to frighten her and keep her from breaking free."

"The old fool! If he rots and feeds the poppies he'll be doing more good than when he was alive."

The bedsprings gave out an alarming creak as the visitor rose suddenly. "This conversation is useless," she said. "I came for the girl's sake, to see if there was anything I could do. The more I thought of my father's concern, the more I was convinced . . ."

". . . convinced that it would be an easy way of appeasing your conscience."

"My conscience did not need appeasing, Miss Clarke. I don't know what you know of my decision to place my father in a home, but I assure you it was not that decision which drove him to take his own life. He was suffering from a terminal disease and spent most of his last hours in great pain."

"I knew nothing about a home for the old fool," Aunt Veeva admitted. "But I know enough about human beings to know that you came here with guilt. You will find no release here. Not from me, and not from the girl. Now—I think you should leave."

"I would like to see the girl."

"That's impossible!"

"Why do you deny me? I only want to speak to her. I know my father was with her the Sunday before he died. I want to know what they talked about. And—and I want to give her this."

I strained to see through the keyhole, but the beds were not situated within view.

"A watch," Aunt Veeva said, as if knowing she was feeding the curiosity of one listening beside the door. "She has her grandfather's watch," she lied. "What does she need with another? With any watch? Time is not so important here."

"It's only a remembrance. I know my father would have wanted her to have it." Her voice had broken and was almost a sob. "It's not a very nice one. It's got a cracked crystal and the gold plating is wearing thin."

I knew that watch well. I had seen it often enough. I had run my fingers over the cracked face, and had polished the gold plate on my sweater sleeve.

"She had a remembrance," Aunt Veeva mumbled. "She has scratches and cuts given to her by the sons of the townspeople when she attempted to attend your father's funeral. What does she need with a man's watch? She'll remember the other things longer. It's those things that will keep her here with me where she belongs."

There was a short lapse of silence.

"I'm sorry," the visitor finally said. "I'm truly sorry. I didn't know."

"Of course, you didn't know. Like your father, you know little of what has gone on here, but you think you can find a solution to our problems. You imagine and invent. I am telling you that the girl will not want the watch. She will not want to see you. Leave us in peace. And tell the others to do likewise."

Mr. Thomas' daughter, Kathryn, moved into my view. She was tall, thin and, I must admit, lovely. Her cheeks were streaked with silent tears. "If the girl ever needs me," she said, "would you tell her I will be waiting."

"If she ever needs you, I will tell her," Aunt Veeva told her without conviction.

"I'll leave the watch anyway," Kathryn said. "I'll leave it on the library table. If she doesn't want it . . ."

"She won't!"

The young woman stopped in the doorway of Aunt Veeva's room. "I did not mean to be unkind, Miss Clarke. I came with the best of intentions."

"Then I suggest you leave with them," Aunt Veeva mumbled.

"Goodbye, then," Kathryn said, and turning, moved out of the room and out of my sight.

I sank away from the keyhole and sat with my back against the door frame. I could remember Mr. Thomas saying: Kathryn—she's all right. She was a good daughter.

For a brief moment—a moment that presented itself and then quickly vanished—I had a feeling of a great weight being lifted from my body. I was also aware that sometime during the night a change had taken place within me. I was not the same girl who had returned home during the storm in fear and frustration. I was someone new, with different thoughts racing through my mind.

CHAPTER TWELVE

Polly was sitting on a milk stool outside the door of her shack when I went for our weekly eggs. She got laboriously to her feet as I came out of the woods and moved forward. As she approached me she lowered her eyes and closed her lips firmly about her snaggled teeth.

"I've got a guest," she told me.

My first instinct was to dash back into the woods until Polly was alone, but she lay a wrinkled hand on my arm to detain me. Craning my neck to see through the open door, I expected to see a sick villager prone on her bed in the midst of some treatment.

Polly read my thoughts. "She's not a customer," she said. "She's come to see you."

"Me!"

"She said her father told her you come to me once a week for eggs," Polly explained.

"I can't see anyone," I said, and tried to shake her hand free. "I *won't* see anyone."

"It could be to your advantage," Polly said in a whisper. Her grasp tightened and her dirty nails dug into the flesh of my forearm. "A girl like you needs friends."

"Let me go!"

But our voices had been overheard. The woman inside the shack called out, then appeared in the open doorway, her thin, pale beauty accentuated by the crumbling shack that formed her background. She wore a white suit with a colorful scarf tied about her neck and thrown back across her shoulder.

Polly released her hold on my arm and I continued to stand and stare at Mr. Thomas' daughter.

"Lillith?" She smiled and I recognized her first resemblance to the man I had loved.

"It's her," Polly said when I did not speak. I could tell by her expression that she thought the woman a fool to expose her teeth so boldly in front of me with my questionable ability. I thought she was going to warn her about the curse of allowing her teeth to be counted, and to prevent this, I stepped forward.

The woman came out of the shack and stood on the block used by Polly as a step. "I came to see you," she said, "but your aunt turned me away." Her voice was kind and gentle.

Reaching into my pocket, my fingers closed about the watch she had left for me on the library table. I held it up for her to see.

Her smile broadened. "I'm glad," she said. "I knew he would have wanted you to have it."

Polly's greedy eyes calculated the value of the watch. Had we been alone, she most likely would have snatched out for it.

I returned the watch to my pocket. "Thank you," I said. "Now I must go." I could feel the muscles of my stomach tightening; my senses screamed for me to run. I could not trust her despite her gentle voice and kind smile.

"Please don't go," she said.

"I must. Aunt Veeva will be angry."

Polly glanced at the young woman. "I told you she would fly away like a frightened bird," she said knowingly. "The child has a devil in her." She grunted her disapproval and moved back to the milking stool where she sat and stretched her crusty legs out into the sun.

The woman gave her a disgusted glance. Then, turning her back on her, dismissed her from her mind. "Lillith, if you'll only stay a moment," she begged. She started forward, but when I stepped back, stopped and nervously clasped her hands together. "Just one minute?" she pleaded.

I nodded.

"I heard about what happened when you tried to come to father's funeral," she said. "I'm so sorry you were hurt."

I automatically rubbed my bruised knuckles.

She sighed helplessly. "It's this valley," she said. "Its advantage is also its nemesis. We are isolated here from many of today's problems, but we must put up with the ignorance of the past."

I remembered Mr. Thomas talking about how smart his daughter had become while she had been away to college in the city. She certainly talked differently from most of the townspeople I had heard from the bridge.

"What I'm trying to say, Lillith, is—well what I would like is for us to be friends. Like you and my father were."

I said nothing.

"I know he met you by the river on Sundays. He told me all about you. About how much he liked you. And how much he worried about you." She lowered her eyes and stared at the ground between us. "I wanted to reason with your aunt," she said, "but that was impossible." The clouded expression that had come to her face with the mention of Aunt Veeva vanished, and she smiled again. "How old are you, Lillith?"

She took my refusal to answer as shyness. "You're a very pretty girl," she said. "There's a great big world outside of this valley. You'd like it there. There are great buildings that touch the clouds, and streets that are so lighted it makes night seem like day."

"Why?"

She laughed.

Polly, sitting with her eyes closed, grunted again.

"So people can see where they are going." Kathryn told me. "There are thousands of people in the city. There are more working in just one building than live in this entire valley. There are movies and the theater." She unfolded her hands and nervously fingered her neck scarf. "Have you ever seen a movie, Lillith?"

"No." I had read about movies in one of Arhen's magazines.

"Well, you must," she said. "You'll like them." Then her face became clouded again. "There are also many doctors in the city," she said. "That's what I wanted to talk to you about." She glanced quickly at Polly. "I understand you suffer from—spells," she said.

"The blackness," Polly inserted. "It's the work of the devil. The child is possessed."

"No!" Kathryn said sharply.

Polly flinched and raised her eyebrows to show her anger at being screamed at.

"Lillith, your spells could be something the doctors could do something about. They could cure you."

Then I understood. Like her father, she was trying to coax me away from Clarke House. Hidden behind her smile and gentle voice, the evil of her intentions had almost escaped me.

"It's just a thought," she said. "On one of my trips to—"

Turning, I fled back into the woods, her voice called after me. I did not stop running until I reached the safety of Clarke Property. Then I threw myself to the ground and lay sobbing. I didn't know why. I had escaped. I was unhurt.

When the tears ended, I rose and walked slowly back toward Clarke House. I felt weak and drained and my body burned with fever.

The words of Mr. Thomas' daughter kept echoing through my head; not the exciting words that described a city, the dark words suggesting I leave the safety of Clarke House, or the request to be my friend. Not those words.

I kept hearing:

You're a very pretty girl.

Nights are filled with sounds, but the familiar sounds seldom wake the sleeper.

It was not the groaning of the old house that awakened me, brought me to my elbows, listening. In some distant corner of the house something had moved and created an unfamiliar disturbance.

Outside, the storm continued after its daytime rest, but it was dying out. The wind was but a whisper through the tree branches; the rain a mere mist, dripping from the waterspouts into the wooden casks below.

I wondered if Aunt Veeva had also been awakened, if she was sitting up in bed waiting for a repeating of the sound. I strained my ear toward her door, but all was quiet within.

The fever was still with me. My forehead was damp with perspiration; my head ached.

After long moments of waiting, the sound came again, softer, more carefully concealed—the sound of an intruder's steps in the rooms above.

I stared at the ceiling, trying to determine from which room the steps had come. In my mind, I retraced the familiar plan of the second floor of Clarke House. Arhen's room was over Aunt Veeva's. The sound had not come from Arhen's room. If my calculations were correct, they came from across the hallway, from the room that had not been opened since that awful day in the past. Someone was pacing the floor of Grandfather Clarke's room!

The steps came again and again, crossing from one side to the other of the locked room. Then, the soft pressure on the floorboards buried by a heavy scraping, something was dragged across the room, something heavy and lifeless.

I could not awaken Aunt Veeva. Before bedtime, she had expressed her anger with me, an anger which stemmed not only from my attempt to attend Mr. Thomas' funeral, but also the appearance of his daughter at Clarke House and her insistence that afternoon on becoming my friend.

Quietly, I turned back the covers and slipped my legs over the edge of the bed. My feet found and slipped into my fur-lined slippers, and I reached for my robe. Crossing the darkened room, I eased the door open and stepped into the library.

A dim, watery light was coming from the library windows. It fell across the floor, stretching the shadows of the furniture to monstrous size. All the doors leading off the library were sensibly closed. I reached back and pulled my own door shut before walking to the center of the room.

Grandfather Clarke's room was large, stretching above my own room to cover the entire area of the library. I continued to stare at the ceiling area as if suddenly expecting my vision to cut through the carved wood and see what moved beyond.

The steps stopped directly above Arhen's massive leather chair. There was a dull thud as if something had been dropped to the floor.

My heart gave a flutter and seemed to stop. My breath came in quick, soundless sobs. The cut on my hand found renewed life. The blood rushed to it, subsided, then returned with a demanding throb for attention.

Above, the steps moved back across the floor. The door opened, its unoiled hinges giving evidence as the intruder passed into the hallway.

The house became hushed.

Without realizing it, I had moved backward and stood against the writing table with its fringed cloth and stacks of dusty books. My fingers touched the pieces of Aunt Veeva's broken figurines; sharp, still waiting the repairman's glue.

I was about to release my breath with a sigh of relief, having stood so long in an absence of sound, but at that moment a light showed beneath the hall door. It moved toward the library, increasing in brightness as the intruder into Clarke House approached the door to the room that hid me.

My bedroom with the safety of its bed was now across the library, the door closed. Aunt Veeva's door was also closed. Had she awakened? Had she heard the final thud from the room above? Was she now sitting upright in bed, calling quietly through the door of my room, hoping to awaken me and warn me to hide?

There was no place in the library to conceal myself except beneath the writing table. The fringe of the cloth would partially hide me. Only if the demon looked closely, let her eyes linger about the floor, would she discover me. I dropped down and slid beneath the cloth, and waited.

Was this the same demon that Aunt Veeva had made so docile on her last visit? The blankets! I had forgotten to burn them. They still lay in a pile beside the kitchen stove.

I could not see the door. The cloth's fringe kept everything but the floor hidden from my sight, but the light told me when the door slid quietly open. Softly, almost entirely without sound, it swung inward and the room was filled with the light of a lantern. I held my breath, pressing tightly against the cut on my hand to prevent crying out with the throbbing pain. I feared the beating of my heart was loud enough to be heard.

The light moved steadily across the room until the demon's legs were within sight. They were covered by a long, white gown which flared outward with each step and clung to the shape of the legs. They moved across the room toward the writing table, and stopped not more than a foot from my cramped form.

I knew the demon had stopped to examine the broken pieces of the figurines she had shattered on her last visit.

Perhaps, I thought, she was wondering what had made her so congenial as to have gathered them from the floor and placed them on the table.

I waited for them to crash to the floor in a moment of rebuke, but, turning away, the demon moved quietly away from the table toward the opposite door—Aunt Veeva's door.

Unable to remain in hiding any longer with Aunt Veeva in danger, I lifted the tablecloth and started to cry out a warning. But the cry died in my throat. I could only stare in disbelief, a heaviness weighting me beyond its support. A chilling shudder passed through my entire body and I turned as cold as one alive can become.

Entering her bedroom, the light held firmly before her, walked a silhouette with silver hair and thin, wasted arms—Aunt Veeva, herself!

CHAPTER THIRTEEN

There was no solace to be found in my betrayal. Better the hateful boys from the town had beaten and killed me; better that than the sight of Aunt Veeva walking healthily across the room, each step grinding the pain of her deception further into the core of my being.

Weakened by the sight and unable to support the weight of my own body, I slid down across the musty carpet much like a thing with no backbone and no control of senses and organs. I lay staring at the light shining beneath her door. It flickered, died, and I was alone in the darkness with the realization of my discovery.

I don't know how long I lay there. Time was unimportant, non-existing. My first feeling—coming in seconds or minutes or hours—was self-pity. It came like a thief and snatched away the thinking part of my mind before I could struggle for self-possession. The struggle would have been useless, the battle lost before it had begun. Tears came from what appeared an endless source.

When I managed to pull myself upright and sat with my head against my knees, still shaken, I noticed that dawn was not far off. Already the light in the library was growing stronger. The storm had passed, and there were morning birds chirping around the sill of the window. This is a new, a different day, I thought. And you, too, Lillith Clarke, are somehow different. Some part of you that the eye cannot detect was caught up in yesterday and did not live through the night.

Beyond Aunt Veeva's door, the quiet of the morning was broken by her heavy sleeping. She turned upon her bed and the springs creaked with her weight, echoing through the recess of the house.

I was filed with a sudden determination. There was a reason for rising from the floor and beginning this new day. That reason lay directly above my head—in Grandfather Clarke's room!

I knew the key hung on a nail just inside Aunt Veeva's door. It had been there since I could remember, a thing to be dusted and looked at with mystery, but never to be removed and used. It was mine for the taking. What would she say if she woke and discovered it gone? What did it matter? My stealing the key could not compare to her deception. I shuddered again with the memory of her walking across the library, her silver mothlike hair glistening in the light of the kerosene lantern.

Something in the room above must have been extremely urgent to have drawn her out of bed to face possible discovery in the middle of the night. The sounds came back to me to claim my thoughts. There had been the steps and the scraping and, finally, the heavy thud as she had let her burden fall to the floor. There had been the creaking of the hinges as she had left the room. I must remember to open the door gently, to slip inside without the merest sound.

I rose and tiptoed to her door. She still breathed heavily, completely lost to sleep. Quietly, I slid the door ajar and let my hand creep around the frame in search of the nail. In my haste my hand came up against the key from beneath. It slipped forward on the nail and fell back against the wall with a hollow, ringing noise that caused me to freeze with panic.

Aunt Veeva tossed on her bed, disturbed but not brought to awareness, not awakened to find my fingers clutching the base of the forbidden key. After a long moment, I pulled my hand back through the door, my fingers clutching the key firmly.

It's mine! The key is mine!

It was an ugly key, rusted and corroded with verdigris. It was rough to the touch, long, stretching the entire length of my small palm. It was warm despite the morning cold.

This key belongs to you, Lillith. Feel its warmth—look at its eye! See the way the design swoops downward like an eyelid, blinking, calling you to its lock! The key holds the secret of Clarke House, the answers for which you have been searching!

I covered the key with my fingers and shook my head as if to clear it. My fever, or a dream—no matter. I had been caught in the delicate spell of the key.

I hurried from the library. At the base of the backstairs, I stepped out of my slippers and pushed them beneath the kitchen table. My first step on the stairs brought a groan, low and threatening. I hesitated. The stairs had not creaked earlier. I had not heard Aunt Veeva as she had descended the stairs. I had only seen the light of the lantern as she had approached the library door. Then I discovered her secret. She had stepped only on the edge of each stair. She had stepped only on the edge of each stair. The wood there was stronger, no weakened by time and traffic.

Cautiously, still testing my theory, I flattened myself against the wall and took another step. There was no sound, only the pounding within my own chest.

The stairwell was dark, but I did not dare a light. Besides, I had begun the climb and could not risk going back for a lantern. I knew Grandfather Clarke's room was opposite Arhen's, and Arhen's room I could find in the black of night. Once on the upper landing, before the door, I moved my fingers over the metal plate until they located the opening for the key. It fit easily without a sound and the lock clicked open at my turn. My mouth was dry, but I managed to coax enough saliva onto my fingers to rub onto the hinges. Then, holding my breath, I gently pushed the door. It swung open easily, if not soundlessly, and I stood staring into the mysterious room.

It was a queer sort of room, bathed in the eerie grey light preceding dawn. The jagged glass of the broken window dripped tears of dew into the dirt of the sill and the curtains, mere fragments, were opened and moving lazily in the morning breeze. To one side of the room sat a massive bed with a canopied top and carved posts; to the other, a gigantic writing desk with the drawers pulled out and the contents in complete disarray. The carpet before the window had suffered obvious abuse at the mercy of the weather. It was stained, covered by a thin film of mildew. The corners of the room from floor to ceiling were in the possession of cobwebs; they, too, glistening with the morning dampness.

I stepped inside and eased the door partially closed behind me, making sure enough space remained for me to slip out again without tempting the rusty hinges a second time. The odor of the room was vile, a thing that had run to meet me when I had opened the door. It lay heavy upon my nostrils, the smell of a dead animal forgotten in one of th4e villager's steel traps.

Just inside the room, I stood and stared about me, not yet brave enough to walk boldly across the floor to the desk or the windows. This is Grandfather Clarke's room, I kept thinking. He lived entirely within these four walls near the end of his life. It was here that he paced back and forth across the Persian carpet and came to the decision to fling himself from the window. It was in this leather chair that he sat day after long day, the door barred to his two daughters and his two bastard grandchildren. I was seized by the brelief that he was somehow present still, a being as invisible as the morning quiet, watching, waiting.

I thought of the room as magic. Surrounding me, it seemed to stretch out in size to encompass more than its mere walled dimensions. Only the massive armoire on the left wall belied the feeling of false space. It sat alone, reaching from floor to ceiling, with carved doors taller than myself and spindle legs that appeared to bow beneath their burden.

Everything else in the room was dwarfed by the sight of the armoire. I turned my back to it and found myself staring into the black mouth of the fireplace. A painting stared back from above the mantel. It was, I thought Grandmother Clarke, and I noted the resemblance to Aunt Veeva. The features were lean, the eyes birdlike, the hair silver, worn in the same twisted bun. Her lips were contorted into an artificial mock smile.

One corner of the room was stacked with books. The sight of them gave me a sense of belonging to the room. Arhen had told me the way Grandfather Clarke had left books for him outside his room. He would find them in the mornings, neatly piled one on top of the other in the order in which he was to read them. He had been caught up in grandfather's love of the printed word, and had passed that love on to me.

Less of a stranger to the room, I turned my attention to the desk. Its contents lay about the top and scattered on the floor. There were notes and receipts and unreadable thoughts scrawled on pieces of yellowed paper. I glanced several times at one that was almost readable before casting it aside. Then I let my fingers search the backs of the drawers, a hiding place I, myself, would choose.

It was there I that I found the diary.

It was small, blue, with a metal lock. The key was in the lock. Why lock anything that is kept in a room which is itself barred to intruders?

The writing was familiar. I had often seen it scrawled across note paper and left in the grocery basket for me to leave at the gate.

This, then, was Aunt Veeva's diary!

Was the little blue book her reason for coming to the room in the middle of the night! Did she come to write down thoughts—to tell of her deception so that she might relieve her conscience!

I turned the cover and began to read.

The first pages were faded, but near the middle was fresh ink.

The Diary:

I warned her often enough.

But she came again.

This time the child was present, trembling on her cot because of the storm. Fortunate that she is so lost in her netherworld of witches and demons that she could easily be sent into hiding.

I faced her alone—all the time knowing what I would do—what I must do!

"You've got to take me back," she said.

I laughed. "Never," I told her. "Because of you I have lost Arhen. I will lose nothing more to you, not even a moment of pity!"

Ah, that sister of mine! She has the stubbornness of our father, the cunning of our mother!

"Arhen!" she cried. "Because of *me* you lost Arhen! Do you intend to carry this charade to your grave? Do you think me as half-witted as my daughter?"

I attempted to ignore her outburst. She had never been one who could reason.

"I have made up my mind," she said, firmly. "You will take me back into the house."

"Never," I said. "You will not return to Clarke House. It belongs to me and you are unwelcome here."

She sank onto the edge of my bed, leaning forward into my face defiantly. Her eyes narrowed to mere slits and her lips curled into a disgusting grin. "I think you are mistaken, sister dear," she said. "I think that Clarke House will again be a haven for me!"

"No!"

"I did not come to beg. I came to bargain."

"Beg or bargain," I told her. "You will not return."

"But I will," she said, wiping the rain from her hair with the tail of my blanket. "Because of our beloved Arhen, you will take me back. Because of Arhen, and because we both know he did not kill the doctor!"

I could only hedge with her, afraid to call her bluff. "Then why didn't you, his mother, come to his defense?" I demanded.

"Why didn't I tell the court that because of her jealousy my sister killed my lover?" She laughed then. "You couldn't stand the thought of my living with him, being held by him, sleeping with him while you lived your twisted little life in this old house with my two bastard children as companions. Why didn't I tell them that you sneaked away from Clarke House in the middle of the night and plunged a knife in his chest while he slept?"

She laughed until my ears ached, until my senses reeled.

"Is that what you would have liked me to say in Arhen's defense?" she demanded. "What a scandal it would have been! You would have had more notoriety than poor Arhen received. And the Clarke estate left to you by our sickly, demented father—what would have happened to that? You'd have lost it," she said. She stood and stared down at me coldly. "I kept silent to protect both of us," she said.

"Arhen loved you," I told her, shocked. "He thought he was protecting you, and you let him go to prison knowing he was innocent."

"Arhen was a fool," she said. "It could have been blamed onto a thief, a stranger. None of us needed to have suffered."

"But one of us did," I reminded her. "Oh, Arhen! How I've regretted not confessing at least to him."

"Do you think Arhen would have taken the punishment for you?" she asked. "Do you delude yourself to that extent?"

"Arhen loved me!"

"Arhen hated you! To him you were more of a social reject than his sister. Do you think he didn't see through those motherly kisses you were constantly smothering on him? You underestimate everyone's intelligence except your own."

"You're heartless!"

"Perhaps," she said, without concern. "But let's not argue. I've come home. Tonight is my homecoming and we should at least tolerate one another. You see, sister dear, we are stuck with each other regardless of how badly you would like to be rid of me."

I was only more determined in my intentions. All the hate I had harbored for her since our childhood rose in my breast. I could hardly breathe with the weight of it.

"Will the child come down tonight?" she asked, crossing to her cot and stretching out.

I told her she would not.

She closed her eyes and I stole a closer look at her. The years had not been kind to her. Her hair had lost its luster. Prettiness had been replaced by plainness. Her face was filled with thousands of tiny lines of age and bad living. Her body was no longer thin, lithe, but had bloated to a disgusting fatness.

"I am tired," she said. "Life isn't easy outside these walls."

Before my breathing had become regular once again she slept.

Echo will not come again!

While she slept, I did what I knew I must. It was quick. She did not know pain.

I wrapped her in one of the blankets from the cot and hid her in the closet. The next day, when the girl was wandering in the woods, I brought her to this room. There are many secrets here—so much of the past hidden away from all except me—hidden in this diary, on scraps of father's paper. Isn't it fitting that this final bit of our hidden history be buried within this room, shielded from obvious view by father's armoire?

I let the book fall closed.

Unable to believe what I had read, I sat staring at the faded blue binding of the diary. If these things were true, the whispers and hatred of the townspeople had been based on fact. I had returned their hate not knowing or believing the tales I had heard from beneath the bridge.

No! No! They could not be true!

Aunt Veeva had somehow managed to get hold of the herbs I told her I could no longer find in the woods. Her writing was a fantasy, the product of a drugged mind.

Then I remembered her deception and my reasoning boggled.

I suddenly thought of Mr. Thomas. I remembered him leaning against a rock, the smoke rising from his pipe to be gobbled by the wind, his eyes boring into me as he spoke. *Too many fantasies, that's your problem. Things you should know about Arhen and your mother and Veeva Clarke!*

No! It could not be true!

—shielded from obvious view by father's armoire.

I turned quickly and stared at the armoire again. It seemed terrifying now, even more massive than before, in complete control of the room. The secret, the truth or fantasy, of Aunt Veeva's diary was hidden behind its carved doors. I needed only to put my fingers through the flowered handles; I needed only to peek inside. If what was written in the diary was true, if it were not merely Aunt Veeva's drugged ramblings, I would know.

But I could not move from the chair.

My mind told my body to rise, my legs to move, but the body only sat shaking, confused by its commands. My head fell forward on the desk top and I pressed my forehead hard against the wood. There was no pain from the pressure, nothing but the whirling sensation within—and a new, odd, creaking sound.

My head shot upward in sudden alarm, my eyes focusing on the door. Slowly it moved inward, the hinges crying a warning that came too late.

In the frame, standing so straight, so still, and so menacing, stood Aunt Veeva, the corners of her mouth turned downward in a curious grimace.

CHAPTER FOURTEEN

We faced one another like two long-time enemies.

Aunt Veeva stood motionless in the doorway, her eyes scanning the room, searching for evidence of the extent of my discoveries; and me, my hand resting on her diary, convinced by the sight of her that what I had read was the truth. Even in my confused mind I could not mistake the facts for fantasy.

"Lillith," she said, softly; and she stepped into the room.

The pressure of her foot was met by a groan from the floorboards. Then miraculously from all about the room the floor began to creak as if from the pressure of invisible steps. At the same time a wind swept through the broken window and the curtain fragments billowed into the room, pulled, it appeared, by unseen hands.

The room is against her, I thought. And she knows—she knows!

Her foot froze and she did not dare a second step.

My eyes turned toward the armoire again. Starting two-eyes widened. "What will you do?" she asked, her voice shaking.

"Arhen," I said. "Arhen is in prison!"

"No! It's not true! Arhen went away. I've told you. Remember? He was carrying on with one of the villager's daughters, the girl in the photograph on his bureau." She waved her hand behind her toward the closed door of Arhen's room. "They ran him out of town," she said. "Remember the night they came? Remember? That's what they did that night. They didn't want him living here." Her gaze turned toward the armoire again. Starting toward me with her arm outstretched, she stopped suddenly, remembering the strange protest of the room. Her arms fell to her sides. "You're only confused," she told me. "It's the effect of the demon. Remember the night of the bad storm? She came for you, Lillith. I destroyed her and put her where you found her. I had to do it. I had to protect you, child."

My hand closed around the diary and I raised it for her to see.

"I know—I know who the demon was," I screamed. "I read it here!"

I flung the diary to the floor at her feet.

She jumped back, staring down at the little blue book as if it were some coiled snake about to strike at her legs. When she raised her head, her face had undergone a change. Fear had vanished with the inescapable knowledge that I now knew her secrets. There was nothing but hate passing between us. *Devil Child*, her eyes seemed to say. *Half-wit!*

"What will you do?" she asked, calmly.

I had not had time to consider my plan. She had discovered me before the full meaning of her diary had been absorbed and understood. "Arhen," I mumbled, more to myself than to her. "I must find someone who will believe me. Someone who will set Arhen free."

She laughed. "You'll find no one to believe you! No one! Never!" She bent and snatched up the diary, clutching it against her breast. "Not without this! Who will believe you? They'll beat you again, that's what they'll do! To the people beyond this wall you're just the half-witted Clarke Girl." Turning, she moved quickly through the door, pulling it closed behind her.

Before I could dash across the room, the key had turned in the lock. The key—my key—had betrayed me. I was a prisoner in the room.

"Half-witted Clarke girl," I heard her say again. "Pound on the door for the rest of your life. You'll not break it down and no one will hear you." Her voice, muffled by the heavy door, began to fade. "You are ironically reunited with your precious mother. Isn't it a fitting—"

Her voice vanished with a final creak of her step on the lower stairs.

When my fist came away from the door and the last echo of my pounding had died, the house was filled with a heavy silence. Even the floor refused to groan beneath my feet as I crossed the room and flung myself on the edge of the dusty bed. The wind had died and the drapes hung straight, unmoving before the broken windowpane. Outside, the morning birds had deserted the trees, they, too, fleeing what in its dense silence could have been the heart of a typhoon, or a closed crypt.

I knew Aunt Veeva must be moving about somewhere below. There was no longer any need for her to pretend paralysis. Perhaps she was burning the diary, destroying the only evidence I could carry to the town in Arhen's defense.

But the other evidence, the body concealed in the armoire—how could she destroy that? And me? Surely she could not allow me to escape and seek the aid of the townspeople. Even if they would not believe me and thought of me as the Devil Child, an accusation against a Clarke would plant a seed, a seed that would not go long without investigation.

Then I thought of Mr. Thomas' daughter, how she had offered me friendship. I would have to find her. She was my only hope.

I remembered the faces of the men who had taken Arhen away and I doubted if they would believe in his innocence. They, after all, had been the ones to lock him in prison for the false crime of murder. It would not be easy to convince them even with proof or Kathryn's help. Still I knew I must try. I must escape from Grandfather Clarke's room and hunt through the town for the one woman who would help me. Arhen had to be set free.

The door was impossible. The heavy wood had been faultlessly constructed to withstand time and a young girl's feeble attempts to force it. Even if such tools as were kept in the shed were at my disposal, I doubt that they would have helped in forcing the door from its frame.

The only other exit was the window. I crossed the room and stood staring down from the great height of the house. It was a long distance to the ground. The bushes which I knew to be taller than I when I stood in the yard were but small weeds from above. And there—there where the grass would not grow over the stones was where Grandfather Clarke had ended his life. Did Aunt Veeva's diary also unveil the mystery of his death? Had he, demented by his loneliness, thought himself a bird and flung himself into the air? Or did the jesting of the hateful boys in the lumberyard have any foundation when they had suggested that he had been pushed?

There was a ledge running the entire length of the front of the house. It created the outside sills of the windows and was supported from beneath by carved figures of nymphs and satyrs, their arms extended above their heads, their backs bent as if bearing the burden of too great a weight.

But the ledge was narrow, offering no more than half a foot of space. It appeared treacherous, still dangerously damp from the morning dew.

I stuck my head through the broken glass and studied the ledge more carefully. None of it seemed to be broken away. At the very end of the house, the giant oak tree rose with its gnarled branches reaching in all directions. One limb was close to the ledge, close enough for my arms to reach. I could cling to the branch, let myself shimmy down the trunk with tomboyish skill and reach the safety of the ground.

Once free, I would run for the town.

Carefully, my heart fluttering in my chest like a bird trying to break free of its cage, I climbed onto the edge of the desk and stuck one leg through the broken glass and placed it firmly on the ledge. With the window frame as a support, I eased my body after it, and was soon free of the room.

I stood quietly staring at the ground far below. My eyes were fixed on the spot where Grandfather Clarke had died. It was like a magnet drawing me forward, down, down to my own death in a like manner. My head reeled and my sight began to blur.

"Don't look down!" I whispered aloud. Shaken to my senses by my own voice, I began to give my instructions. "Hold your head back against the side of the house. Look straight out beyond the wall. Don't look down! Now! Move your feet slowly! Slowly!"

I could feel the pressure of my feet on the ledge. Only my heels and half the soles were secure; my toes, I knew, were suspended on empty air far above the ground. I moved sideways two, three steps. Then I stood still, allowing my fluttering heart to catch up with my frightened body. The dizziness in my head subsided. I had begun! There was no stopping now. Turning, I examined the ledge to the end of the house. It seemed a great distance, greater than it had from inside.

From far out in the fields came the barking of a dog. I used the sound as a wedge against my fear. It was something to cling to, to concentrate on. It was a hunting dog, I thought. Its master had probably made a kill, a pheasant, perhaps, and the dog was calling out the position of the lifeless carcass.

I took another step; then two.

Arhen had to be set free! Only I could do it. I, who loved him more than any other person in the world, would be the one to free him.

Three! Four! Five!

The end of the house was closer now, but a more difficult task loomed ahead. I had not noticed the waterspouts. They stood out from the side of the structure at a level with my chest; gargoyle heads, their mouths still dripping the remains of last night's rain. To pass them I would have to swing my body around them, losing the safety of the wall at my back. For one brief moment I would be relying on the strength of my arms to support me.

Five—six steps more.

My hand reached one of the creature's heads. It was cold to the touch, but its support meant temporary safety. I clung to its neck and took several deep breaths of air into my lungs. My chest ached and my face felt hot, burning with the return of the fever. I held one hand under the gargoyle's mouth, caught the raindrops, and rubbed them on my face. They were instantly cooling and my bravery returned.

It was then that I became conscious of eyes upon me. Turning, I saw Aunt Veeva. She was leaning out of Grandfather Clarke's broken window, her elbows on the sill, her eyes wide with amazement. The wind had caught her hair and tore it loose from its bun. It whipped about her face like the snake-hair of Medusa, the effect causing me to clutch even tighter to the neck of the waterspout and utter a high, useless whimper of frightened surprise.

"Lillith! Child, come back!"

I continued to cling to the gargoyle, shaking my head violently in protest to her request.

"Come back, Lilly! Before you fall!"

"No!" I cried. "I must save Arhen!"

"There's no need," she said. "Are you listening, Lillith? There's no need. Arhen is downstairs! Arhen has come home!"

She would not deceive me again. I would not be duped with this new invention. Locking both hands over the waterspout, I swung my body away from the building. The arch which was to have brought me safely to the opposite side of the gargoyle was ill-timed. My feet struck the underside of the ledge and I swung back to hang helplessly. Terror seized me. It was the terror and the knowledge that Aunt Veeva was watching that gave me the strength to pull myself back onto the ledge, back to where I had been standing with the passing of the waterspout to be attempted yet another time.

"Lillith, Arhen is waiting! He's asking for you! Come back, child."

"Come back to be pushed? No," I screamed. "You're lying. Everything you've told me has been a lie." I began to whimper softly. "And I trusted you."

"I'm not lying." She persisted. "It's true, Lillith! It's God's truth!"

"Lies!" I screamed. "Arhen is in prison! Arhen is suffering for your crime."

Her face was contorted by desperation. She kept peering nervously over her shoulder as if expecting someone to suddenly appear in the room behind her.

Then, from deep within the house, from the very heart of Clarke House, came the sound of a familiar voice calling my name.

Arhen!

CHAPTER FIFTEEN

Was this my brother?

He sat in Arhen's chair, this man, his feet resting on Arhen's footstool in the old, familiar way, with his legs crossed at the ankles and slightly raised, his hands resting on one knee.

But there was something about him that held me in the doorway, something strange, unremembered that would not allow me to rush forward in a joyous greeting.

He wore trousers and a shirt of a drab grey coloring. Both were splattered with mud. One sleeve of his shirt had been torn away and the underarms were stained by perspiration. He also had a beard. Particles of earth and burrs from the fields clung to its black, unkempt hair. Dark and thick as the beard might have been, it did not entirely hide the scar across his right cheek. Red and frightening, it peeked through the heavy growth as if defying concealment. His eyes were the black eyes of Arhen. They held the expression of a man who had fought a long and bitter battle and was not preparing to concede defeat.

Aunt Veeva had moved swiftly into the library and had gone to stand beside the window, her thin fingers laced through the wide weave of the curtains. My only condition in coming in the ledge was that she would walk down the stairs a good distance ahead of me. This she had done, a new look of fear in her eyes as she had glanced at me over her shoulder. With Arhen waiting for us below, she had become the trapped instead of the trapper. It was I who would hold the upper hand. Now, pulling back the curtain and glancing into the yard, she appeared remarkably cool and collected. There was no tremble to her hand, no visible nervousness.

"Come in, child," she said without looking in my direction.

I stayed beside the door, undecided. "Arhen! Is it you?"

He stirred. His feet left the stool and planted themselves firmly on the floor. He seemed to want to stand, but he did not. Some weight held him to the chair's edge, his black eyes fixed, unblinking, on me. "Lillith," he said, softly, and held out his arms to me as only Arhen could have done.

Suddenly, I was flooded with the greatest joy I had known. "Arhen!" I cried, and running forward, threw my arms about his neck. "It's you! It's really you, Arhen!"

He held me against his chest, the mud and seat of his clothing damp against my cheek. "Yes, little sister, it's me," he whispered his voice deep, weary, and hardly audible. "Did you think you would never see me again?"

I was unable to answer. Words would not pass my constricted throat. I continued to cling to him for fear if I released him he would vanish as suddenly as he had appeared.

"You've grown," he said, suddenly holding me away from him for closer examination. "You are almost a grown woman. My little Lillith, almost a woman." Laughing, he pulled me back into the curve of his body and tightened his grasp. "My God!" he cried. "It's been so long!"

"So very long," I mumbled.

"When I went . . . away . . . you were still wobbly on your feet—no more than a baby."

Aunt Veeva stirred behind me. She came away from the window and crossed to stand beside the writing table. I could hear her fingers drumming softly on the polished top, and I could sense her eyes upon us.

I pulled away from my brother, standing so that both he and Aunt Veeva were within eyesight. "Arhen," I began. "I must tell you—"

Aunt Veeva stepped forward. "Not now, child," she interrupted. "This is not time for talk that can be postponed. Arhen is tired and hungry."

Arhen rose from his chair. Ignoring the two of us, he began to pace about the library, picking up things from the tables, examining the, setting them down again. After circling the entire room, he came back again to his chair and sank onto the edge. His eyes continued to roam the room as if his hunger for familiar objects could not be satisfied.

"Arhen, I—"

Arhen turned to me, clasped my shoulders between his powerful hands, and laughed. "Remember the time I found you crying in the woods?" he asked.

When I did not answer, his hands came away from my shoulders and his fingers gently brushed the skin beneath my moist eyes. "You were so easily frightened," he remembered.

His touch like his voice was kindly intended, but his fingers were rough. Looking down at his hands, I saw the dampness from my eyes trapped in the deep crevices of his fingers. His hands were no longer the hands I had sought for comfort. They were not the young, strong hands he had offered so willingly, but the hands of a man old before his time, hands as old as those of Mr. Thomas.

"Why do you cry?" he asked.

It was Aunt Veeva who answered. "She's feverish," she told him. "She caught her death of cold in the storm."

"The storm," he repeated, the corners of his mouth beginning to form his old smile. "Then you are no longer afraid of the rain?"

"No," I admitted. "I am no longer afraid—of the rain."

"Good." He rose once more and, crossing to the window, pulled back the curtains and looked out. "They won't miss me until the men come in from the yard," he said. "I have only a short time."

As if called upon, the clock struck eight.

"Half and hour at the most," he continued. "Then I must leave. I must cross the river and reach the base of the mountains before I am missed." He turned to Aunt Veeva. "I'll need money," he told her. "As much as you can spare."

Aunt Veeva hurriedly left the room. I could hear her in the bedroom taking the metal box containing her money from the trunk.

Accepting what my mind wished to reject, I crossed the room to face Arhen. "You escaped," I said. His clothes were the clothes of a prisoner, the clothes of those restless men who moved behind the bars of the building on the hill beyond the river. Arhen had come home, but only in flight.

He did not speak, but merely stood looking down at me, his eyes saying he wished it were not true. They told me he wished he had come home to stay. Then, turning away from me, he moved to the desk and stood leaning forward, both palms flat on its surface. "They'll come here after me," he said finally. "You'll have to face them again, Lillith. You'll have to pretend you've never seen me." His brow furrowed ion anger. "They'll be like wild men. It will be the same as before."

"No!" I cried. "Let them take Aunt Veeva! Not you! Aunt Veeva! She's the one they want! She killed the doctor!"

"Oh, dear," she said from behind me. "I had hoped you would be spared the truth!"

I spun about and stared at her as she entered the library, the metal box tucked under her arm, the lid open and a roll of green bills between her fingers.

"But, alas, you can see, Arhen, she's no better than before. Maybe even worse. She's continually gone further and further into that private world of hers where there is no distinction between reality and fantasy." She set the box down on the desk in front of Arhen. "There was nothing I could do with her after you left. Nothing! She even swears I killed your mother." She pushed the roll of bills into Arhen's shirt pocket. Looking at me, she shook her head in a hopeless manner. "There are times when I think she is becoming normal. I hope and pray, but you can see my prayers have gone unanswered." She sighed.

Arhen was watching me, but his eyes were not seeing. He was remembering a smaller, a younger Lillith Clarke who had been afraid of rain and had sworn she was a witch. "I thought when you mentioned the storm," he said, "that all of that was in the past, something she had outgrown."

"Arhen!" I screamed. "It's true!" So this then was her plan. She hoped to discredit me, to use that dead, innocent part of me that she had created to win her battle of deception. "It's true, Arhen! I read it in her diary!"

"Lillith!" Aunt Veeva cried. "Stop this foolishness at once!"

"It's true!" I continued to protest.

Arhen turned away from us. He stood facing the wall, his head slumped forward into his shoulders. Aunt Veeva moved to his side and laid her hand gently across his arm.

But not before she gave me a look of triumph—a look that said she had won and it was useless for me to persist.

"I'll take care of her, Arhen," she promised. "I'll do the best I can."

"No!" I sprang forward, grabbing Aunt Veeva by the arm and shoving her away from Arhen. She knocked into the desk, clung to its side to keep from falling to the floor. "Come with me Arhen! Come with me to Grandfather Clarke's room!"

Arhen was confused, stricken by my fit of anger against Aunt Veeva, but weakening, I could tell, by my determination to prove myself sane.

And then the spells by which I am afflicted began to claim the thinking part of my mind. I could sense the vertigo and the clouding of my sight. I began to babble: "Upstairs . . . the armoire . . . mother! . . . she has killed mother!"

Aunt Veeva pulled herself to her feet. Her eyes were fixed on Arhen's face. She was studying his dark expression in an effort to judge his reaction to the half-coherent sentences gushing from my mouth.

"Arhen, she's not herself! It was the excitement of seeing you," she said. "She's not strong—the poor child. She's not at all well."

In a last effort to convince my brother, I wrapped my arms about his waist, and cried: "Arhen, please!"

There was so little time. Soon the men from the town would come with their dogs pulling at their leashes. They would track Arhen as if he were an animal. He would never reach the mountains.

"Not well at all," Aunt Veeva repeated. "We've had doctors, of course," she lied, "but there is nothing they can do. Hereditary, they said. Some unknown gene that feebles the mind."

I tightened my hold on Arhen. I was fighting two battles: the battle to retain my senses and not give in to my spells, and the battle to convince Arhen of my discovery. But words became impossible, scrambled in my mind. I could only keep repeating: "Please, Arhen! Please!"

Aunt Veeva came forward. "Arhen, you can't waste any more time," she said. "The river is high. The footbridge may be under water and you'll have trouble crossing. You must hurry, Arhen."

"Please, Arhen."

Aunt Veeva dared not come too close to me for fear I would turn on her suddenly. She stood at a safe distance, one arm outstretched toward Arhen. "Arhen, time is the important thing."

But Arhen was listening to neither of us. He was hearing other sounds—the sound he had dreaded. He was hearing the wail of the siren from the prison as it warned the townspeople that a prisoner had escaped. It was not yet eight-thirty, but they had missed him. They had counted the cattlelike heads of the prisoners, and someone had announced:

Arhen Clarke is missing!

Reaching down and removing my arms from his waist without the slightest effort, Arhen stared into my face. His eyes were filled with pity. His lips formed words he could not speak and his eyes made promises he could not keep. He moved me to one side, where, shaken by my defeat, I stood silently while, with a nod to Aunt Veeva, he hurried from the room.

Presently, we heard the closing of a distant door.

Aunt Veeva, sighing, slumped against the desk, exhausted but victorious. Her breath was coming in small gasps, her hands now trembling since the danger had passed.

It was the sight of her that brought me to my senses.

"Arhen!" The cry tore from my throat and must still have echoed in the house behind me as I ran from the library in pursuit of my brother.

Outside, the wind was blowing the dead leaves of the oak trees against the side of the house. The gate, left open, swung freely on its creaking hinges. Darting through it, I stood on the knoll overlooking the woods.

"Arhen! Come back!"

My cries were caught up by the wind and hurled back against the house to lie unheard among the dead leaves.

Climbing the barbed wire fence, I ran after Arhen, forgetting the ruts of the field, falling, rising and falling again.

"Come back, Arhen! There's no reason to run. For God's sake, come back!"

But he ran in among the trees and vanished.

With one last effort, I screamed his name. Then, falling to the ground, I could not rise again.

CHAPTER SIXTEEN

T he siren continued at regularly spaced intervals.
It found me where I lay and drove fear for
Arhen further into my heart. I prayed that my ears
would suddenly become some mystical sponge which would
soak up the sound and prevent it from hurrying on to every
corner of the valley. There would not be a townsman who
would not stop his work, look with growing excitement to
the building on the hill, and then run for his weapon. The
women would come to their doors, wiping their hands on
their aprons, and call their children into the protective sight
of one room. They would watch silently as their husbands
took their guns from the walls and loaded their hunting sacks
with shells. They would wonder at this masculine weakness

which was responsible for the frightening expressions in their men's eyes. The dogs would be barking; they, too, impatient for the hunt to begin. The children, still huddled together in one corner, would cover their ears with their hands, their minds trying to puzzle out the effect of the siren on the adults. The dogs at their heels, the men would leave, and the women would bolt their doors. Even with the doors and windows securely locked, they would not feel safe, not with the siren finding entry into their homes through the smallest cracks. They would wonder about the safety of their men, and the men would wonder if they would be the one to catch the fugitive and claim the generous reward offered by the prison.

No one would concern themselves with the fate of the prisoner. No man had succeeded in escaping the valley.

Mr. Thomas had told me that it was because all the men who had climbed the walls to freedom had been strangers, men brought from the cities to be confined in the building on the hill. None of them had any knowledge of the forest or the complexities, the seasonal moods of the mountains. They were city men, he had said, men who were accustomed to a different jungle.

Arhen might have a chance, I thought. He knew the forest and the mountains. He was not like the other men who had sought freedom.

He had a change if I could help him. He needed time—
time to reach the safety of the mountains—time to lose his
scent in the creek beds so that the dogs would be unable to
track him.

Arhen needed me!

But could I face the men? And even if I stood up to them,
would they believe me when I attempted to send them in
some opposite direction?

If the dogs got him! I shuddered. Many were the times
I had seen them at the heels of a wounded deer, their teeth
tearing at its throat in an effort to bring it to the ground.

I got to my feet and stood staring at the spot where Arhen
had disappeared into the woods. I knew he would take my
path. He would pass the lean-to he had built for me, and, if
for but one fleeting moment, he would remember the day he
had found me there, he would remember me clinging to his
neck, and he would know that my love was as strong today as
it had been then.

The footbridge would be ahead of him with the swollen
river rushing over its sides and trying to drag him into the
current. Beyond the footbridge lay the marshes, beyond the
marshes, the mountains. The mountains were his friends. If
he could reach them, he would reach freedom.

Turning from the woods, I stared back at Clarke House. I
studied the familiar windows, knowing what lay behind each. I

examined the peaked roof and the brick fireplace as if seeing them for the very first time. I was now an outsider. There was no longer a bond between the house and me. My feeling of belonging, my pride, had vanished. The house was nothing more than an ugly structure, no castle as I had imagined, but a decadent eyesore. When there had been the hope that Arhen would come home, the house had been my companion in waiting, but now that he had returned and gone again and would never return, the house was no more than a shell. It stood alone, waiting only to crumble.

The siren sounded again. Its wail seemed more desperate, more demanding of notice. Precious little time had passed since its warning had first broken the morning quiet, but already the men would be gathering in the village. They would soon be hurrying along the river path toward Clarke House, their anger building, their dogs tugging at their leashes in an effort to run ahead.

With one last glance at Arhen's path of flight, I ran toward Clarke House, the siren blaring across the valley to spur me on.

I would face the hateful ones. I must make them believe my lies or whatever garbled speech I could manage.

CHAPTER SEVENTEEN

The men were approaching along the river path.

Their voices, mingled with the excited baying of the dogs, preceded them and scaled the walls of Clarke House as though it did not exist.

I could see the gate from my hiding place in the bushes beside the front porch steps. The crossbar was firmly in place and fortified by a timber I had managed to wedge into the ground. It would take time for them to break it down—and time was what Arhen needed.

Somewhere in the house, Aunt Veeva must have been watching from a window, she, too, gripped by panic at the approaching voices. I did not think she had seen me as I had barred the gate and taken the timber from the shed to fortify it. She probably thought I continued to chase along the forest path in pursuit of Arhen, still screaming her guilt. Never would she suspect that her niece was hiding beside the steps waiting to face the hateful townsmen she feared so much. Not Lillith, she would be thinking. Not even for Arhen.

The dogs reached the gate first. They scratched and howled about the cracks until the men arrived and kicked them aside. The aged wood of the gate began to vibrate with the pounding of their fists.

"We know you're in there, Clarke! Come out! You haven't got a chance!"

Although their voices called for him to show himself, I knew by their tones that it was the last thing they hoped for. If Arhen should suddenly step from the house, cross the yard and throw open the gate, the hunt would be ended. Their excitement would die unspent. There would be no tracking through the forest, no hunt, no possibility of any one man claiming the reward for his capture.

"Come out, Clarke!"

I crouched, waiting silently, staring out through the leaves of the bushes, my eyes fixed on the gate. The timber was strong. They would not break it easily, but eventually the crossbar would snap and the timber would lose traction in the earth and slip away. The gate would be opened. What I would then do I could not imagine. My mind was smothered by fear of the angry men. I could not formulate a plan.

Then my breath caught in my throat and my heart skipped a beat. The head of one of the men rose above the wall. His arms clutched at the concrete and he slowly pulled his body to the top. There he stood, legs planted firmly apart on the top bricks, and stared into the yard; unafraid, his eyes appraised the house. He was a giant of a man, familiar. When he turned his head to speak to the men below, I recognized him as the logger I had seen from beneath the bridge, the man with the spiked shoes who had said that Clarke House should be torn down so a man would not have to walk three extra miles to the mill. He had come, this giant of a man, to execute his wishes. He leaped into the garden, kicked the timber from the gate, and raised the crossbar.

The gate swung open and the men and dogs swarmed into the yard. They approached the house slowly with hunters' caution. When they stood almost directly in front of me, they stopped and stared up at the front door.

I hunched further down into the protection of the bushes.

The man from bridge held up his hand and his companions fell silent. The dogs continued to bark until they, too, sensing the power of the man, sought the familiar legs of their masters, and were silent.

"Arhen Clarke!" His voice was the voice of a great bull, angered, bellowing a warning before its charge. His legs, like the stumps of a tree, appeared to be rooted in the ground. His head was thrown back, his teeth showing white against the darkness of his skin. His arms were bare despite the morning cold, the sleeves of his shirt rolled up about thick, hairy arms. "Arhen Clarke! Come out!"

When there was no answer, I knew they would tear away the door. They waited, and their anger mounted with each passing moment of silence.

It was time for me to rise and face them. It was time for me to prove that I was made of stronger fiber then either Arhen or Aunt Veeva believed. Taking a deep breath of air into my lungs, I shifted my feet to a position for rising, but as I prepared to reveal myself there was a murmur among the men. Each took a step backward, their eyes fixed on the door like senseless children, their determination dragged from them by whatever they saw.

I lifted my head and found myself staring up at Aunt Veeva. She stood on the edge of the porch glaring down at the men. Her hair hung loose across her breasts, silver against the black of her best robe. Her face was white, her mouth set with all the hate she had carried for the townspeople since her childhood. Even from directly below her. I could see the glint in her hawklike eyes, the downward curl of her lips. She truly looked the witch the townspeople thought her to be.

Of all of the men, only the logger had not yielded his ground. He still stood firmly rooted to his spot, his feet parted to support his great body. "We've come for your nephew," he said. His voice was less coarse, his attitude more that of a request instead of a command.

Aunt Veeva took a step forward. Her robe hung over the edge of the porch boards. She fixed her gaze directly on the man. He had challenged her and she would not back away.

"You are a stranger," she said. She spoke the word "stranger" as if it were intolerable. "You dare to break the gate of my house and trample my garden! Heathens, the lot of you!" She waved her hand in an all-encompassing gesture, causing some of the men to step even further away from the porch.

The logger's face reddened. "We're sorry about the gate," he mumbled, "but it was barred and braced by a timber."

"As it should be," Aunt Veeva cried.

"You can't go on defying the town," the logger said. "Perhaps, the ignorant and the superstitious are afraid of you, but I'm neither of those. Your nephew—send him out!"

The men were watching the logger closely. He had made himself their self-appointed leader. Now he was expected to face this creature they had lived in awe of for years. He would either succeed in conquering her, or they would be forced to turn away, beaten, and recoup their determination. Their demands of the logger were in their eyes, mingled with years of superstition concerning anyone connected with Clarke House. They would willingly surround the grounds, but unless Aunt Veeva was proven no more than a mere woman they would not assault the house itself.

The logger was aware of their fears. He knew their loyalties as well. He knew the woman on the porch might possibly destroy their support of him. It was something he had obviously not counted on facing. He looked the type to willingly go into battle with any man, but facing a woman, especially a woman like Aunt Veeva, had chipped away some of his bravado. "Your nephew had escaped," he said. "We've come to take him back."

"Is that why you broke my gate?" Aunt Veeva asked with pretended surprise. "You think my nephew is here? You think he is hiding behind my skirts?" She laughed and the sound of that laughter sent a shiver through me. "Well, stranger, he is not here," she said. "Not any longer. No murderer, not even a Clarke, will find refuge in my house!"

I could not believe my ears.

The men began to mumble among themselves.

"Then he's been here?" the logger demanded, holding up his hand for silence.

I stared up at Aunt Veeva. She had turned even against Arhen to save herself. She was patronizing the townsmen, clutching her Bible to her breast so that they might see and believe her lies.

"Yes, he's been here," she told them. "But I turned him away. I will hide no murderer in my house."

I knew she had mesmerized the mob. They were hers. She could mold them into whatever belief struck her fancy. She could convince them of her innocence as easily as she had convinced me that I had been a product of the darker side of life.

The logger stepped to the porch. If I had stretched out my arm, I could have touched him. He was perspiring heavily, the sweat standing out on his hairy bear's arms. "How long ago?" he asked. "Which way did he go?"

"While you were breaking my gate down he was crossing the river at the footbridge," she told him.

"He's headed for the mountains," one of the men shouted. "He knows them well. I've hunted there with him in the old days. We'll have one bad time catching him."

"But we can catch him," the logger assured the crowd. "We'll head him off. We'll go back for the cars and surround the marshes. They're high because of the rain. He'll not get through them easily. We'll have all the time we need."

The anger of the mob had returned twice as strong, and Aunt Veeva had done it. She with her bible and her lies had built the men into a feverish pitch of excitement. They began to turn away and call their dogs into action.

"Wait!" she suddenly screamed.

Everyone stopped and turned back to the porch.

"He's armed," she lied. "He'll shoot any man who stands between him and freedom."

"We'll shoot first!" someone cried.

The call was picked up by the other men. They raised their rifles above their heads.

"Shoot first!"

With a cry that rose above the din of their chant, my eyes wild with desperation, I leaped from my hiding place in the bushes. "It's not true!" I screamed. "It's all lies! Wait! It's not true!"

The dogs, startled, ran up to the bushes and began barking at my legs. Several of the men had swung their rifles into position for firing, thinking, I suppose, that it was Arhen who was springing up before them.

"She's lying!" I cried. "Arhen's inside! He's inside! She's hiding him!"

Aunt Veeva, surprised by my sudden appearance at her feet, had jumped back against the door. She was staring at me in disbelief, alarmed that her spell over the townsmen had been suddenly broken. She stepped forward again, fighting to regain her hold. She waved her hands violently, screaming: "This child is feebleminded! You all know it. You call her the Devil Child. She doesn't know what she's saying. She has black fits! Don't listen to her. I'm telling you the truth. While you hesitate, Arhen is getting away."

The men looked from me to Aunt Veeva and back again. Her cries were becoming incoherent. Her body shook violently and she seemed on the verge of collapse.

"He's upstairs!" I yelled. "Hiding in Grandfather Clarke's room!"

Her sudden scream told me that I had won. I had broken her spell. The men believed *me*.

Struck on the head by the Bible Aunt Veeva flung at me, I pitched forward to the ground as she turned and ran through the door. She slammed it behind her, and I heard the bolt drawn into place. The corner of her robe had caught on the frame and showed on the outside of the door like the skin torn from an animal.

The men ran forward, threw their weight against the door, yelling. Aunt Veeva had managed to build their anger. Now it was turned against her. The dogs were frantic. One jumped onto my chest and snarled down into my face. Knocking it away, I got shakily to my feet.

I had done right. Arhen would be safe. The men would break down the door. They would find the body in the armoire and everyone would then believe me when I told them of Aunt Veeva's guilt and Arhen's innocence.

I had won!

The butt end of a rifle was shoved through the window pane of the library. It shattered the glass which fell away to allow one of the men to be hoisted through the opening. His hands were cut and began to bleed, but he did not seem to notice. He lifted his companion in behind him and the two of them disappeared into the heart of the house.

I did not realize how weak I had become due to the strain of facing the men until a dog brushed against my legs and I had to fight to retain my balance. My head was in a whirl. The excitement of the men, their screams as they assaulted the house acted on me like a drug. Finally, unable to stand any longer, I staggered to the wall and crawled into the tall grass.

I heard the door give way with a mighty groan, and men and dogs hurried into the house. What followed was a nightmare of sounds and sights, windows shattering as furniture was thrown into the yard, shouts, the dogs' barking, and the occasional explosion of a gun.

Then the sounds themselves seemed to end as if broken. The ominous silence that followed brought me to my knees to see men, their arms filled with articles from the house, pouring back into the yard. They were followed by a thin stream of smoke that escaped from the tops of the windows and doors and rose lazily to hang in a blue haze above the peaked roof. It became heavier and darker, and the men, motionless now, stood staring up at the window above, waiting it seemed, for Aunt Veeva or Arhen to show themselves and plead for help.

The burly logger stepped out of the group and, cupping his hands to his mouth, began to scream up at the window. "Fire! Clarke, for God's sake, come out now! Bring your aunt out! The house is burning!" His clothes were torn, his hair matted with blood from a cut on his forehead.

The other men remained silent. They seemed to have become once again nothing but dumb sheep. Their anger had been spent. Their old fears and superstitions returned. They watched the window, eyes wide with wonder, and waited.

The flames licked through the library window and rose red and orange along the side of the house. The limbs of the oak tree caught at the fire and passed it along its branches, content to sacrifice itself with the house.

The logger was in a state of frenzy. He attempted to rush back into the house, but the heat of the flames prevented his entry. Returning to the yard, he stood screaming above the roar of the fire. "Clarke, don't be a fool! Save your aunt!"

A new sound filled my ears. The earth seemed to be shaken from running feet. The townspeople began to appear from all directions. Boys climbed the walls for a better view. Women, their children clinging to their skirts, crowded inside the gate and formed a line along the wall like spectators at some sports event. Their eyes were wide with the same fearful expression they had questioned in their husbands earlier that morning. The men, moving backward away from the flames and heat, joined their wives and were silent for the most part.

"We're burning ourselves a witch," one of the men told his wife. She gave a meaningless cry of protest, but refused to avert her gaze from the burning house. Her child, too young to understand, clutched at her legs and attempted to hide its face.

The logger—the one-time leader—covered his eyes with his hands and ran blindly through the gate he had opened for the crowd. He made for the river path along which he had come so bravely only minutes before. The cheering of the crowd, the false cries of pity from the women had drained him of all strength. He could not helplessly face the upstairs window and know that a woman and her nephew had chosen to burn rather than face them. He was no longer a bull, but a weakling, not as strong in the eyes of the townspeople as the smallest of their children who stood and cheered and did not turn away.

Suddenly, with the force of an explosion, the flames shot out from the house and then quickly drew inward to engulf the whole of the upstairs. Within moments Clarke House was no more than a charred frame.

I had been forgotten by the townspeople. I lay in the tall grass as unnoticed as the articles they had carried from the house. My hair and arms had been burned by cascading cinders, but I was unaware of pain.

When the house frame collapsed the people began to drift silently away. I watched them go, walking slowly up the dirt road and glancing occasionally over their shoulders as if to make certain they were not followed by some vengeful spirit that had survived the flames.

People came throughout the day to stand and stare at the remains of Clarke House. I remained in the tall grass until darkness fell—then I crept out to keep warm by the still glowing cinders.

EPILOGUE

All the white pages are filled, the pencils dulled. They told me I must write of Aunt Veeva and the demons—and of Arhen—and I have done so to please my new friend.

Kathryn came to me when Clarke House was no more than cooling ashes. She took my hand and led me away to a place where it is quiet and peaceful. When I did not know where to turn, she found me.

She has all the gentleness of her father's soul and the beauty of his mind. Sometimes when the sunlight catches her hair just right I am reminded of an old man sitting lazily at the river's edge, and I am filled with a quiet peace.

We have talked of Arhen, and I believe she understands better than myself that Aunt Veeva did not die without claiming a share of victory. When two skeletons were found in the remains of Clarke House it was assumed they were Aunt Veeva and Arhen.

But we have decided to let Aunt Veeva retain her share of victory. We shall not identify my mother's remains. Arhen, thought dead, will remain so to me. I shall not see him again.

We both have found a measure of freedom.

Spring has come again. The forest grass is green and soft and flowers bloom along the creek. I long to feel the earth damp beneath my body and to lie and watch clouds forming mysterious shapes in the sky, but I shall never again let their reality become hidden beneath my fantasies.

On the knoll where Clarke House once stood, a blackened fireplace stands alone. It looks as if it has stood thus for many years and not just through the changing of two seasons. It will be a constant reminder of those dark days behind me and of the future I am now free to build.

THE CROP

Dorothy Wade stepped out on to the porch, shielded her eyes with her hands and examined the noonday sky. Curious dark shadows passing over the windows had brought her hopefully from the kitchen. But now, blinking under the glare of the sun, the sight of the one lone cloud moving off on a high wind brought an abrupt end to hope, and discouragement returned, an even heavier burden.

Leaning back against the doorframe, she stared out beyond the picket fence and cornfields at the cloud of dust rising along the horizon. Jack was coming home from market—and in a hurry, too, by the looks of the disturbance the old car was making on the dirt road.

It wasn't like Jack to push the car. He spent most of his Sundays tinkering around with the old heap, trying he said, to make it last another year. Well, she thought, it would never last at that pace.

With a weary sigh, she stepped off the porch and into the yard. She filled a can with water from the outside tap and sprinkled it sparingly around the cracked ground beneath her snowball bush. The prized plant, despite the favoritism of daily watering, had begun to die. Like the other shrubs, it was turning brown, its leaves drooping like wilted cabbage.

Other summers the yard had been a lush Eden of green grass and blooming flowers. Roses had filled the trellis and marigolds had lined the walkway in a profusion of color. But not this year. The Fresno Court House had never before recorded so hot a year; and to add to the heat, there was the water shortage.

Some said it was the city folks who were to blame, letting their faucets run continuously out of anger against the sky-rocketing prices. But that didn't make sense. City people were peculiar, it was true, but they, too, had to eat, and without the farmers where their food come from?

The heat and dry irrigation ditches had caused the death of most of the crops. What precious vegetables had survived the first few weeks of the heat wave were not selling for unheard of prices in the cities. Rumor had it that tomatoes were selling for $2 apiece, lettuce at $5 a head, and squash, if it could be found at all, for $8. All fresh vegetables except corn had become delicacies.

Corn! It was unnatural the way the corn had survived—had even seemed to thrive on conditions that had killed off the other crops.

Dorothy dropped the watering can and stood looking out past the fence at the huge boulder sitting in the middle of the cornfields. In all her years on the farm she had never become accustomed to the sight of the boulder. In the entire valley as far as the eye could see, there was only one rise in the level land, and that was the boulder. It had been there since before memory of any settlers, a stone sentinel standing watch over the flatlands. Its size made the corn look half its height.

The corn! Corn had been their major crop. They had had one field of cucumbers and another small plot of vegetables for their own use. Both were now black with rotting plants, but the corn grew on, defying nature.

She felt a deep resentment for the corn. She resented its survival over her snowball bush and her marigolds and over the garden that was to have fed them for the year. She resented the way it pressed up against the fence as if it had the unquestioning right to claim the burnt-out yard surrounding the house.

Defiantly, she crossed the yard and stooped to break off the corn leaves protruding through the pickets. She clutched a handful of the leaves, pulled and twisted, but they would not tear away from the stalks. She backed away, staring at the head-high corn in disbelief. All her strength had been useless against the plants.

"It's crazy," she mumbled aloud, attempting to shake the fright that had seized her. She started forward for a second assault against the corn, but stopped suddenly, her eyes fixed on the empty flower bed that normally would have been filled with yellow cannas. Tiny green sprouts had begun to force their way up through the parched soil.

The corn had crossed the fence!

The old car rattled up before the front gate and came to an exhausted halt. Queenie leaped from the window and dashed off through the fields, barking with the excitement of homecoming.

With a last look at the sprouts invading her flower bed, Dorothy hurried to the gate. Jack had climbed out of the car and was unloading the empty crates. His face was drawn, his movements those of a man forced to face defeat.

"The corn's in the yard," she told him. "In the flower beds."

He glanced up at her, then quickly back to his work as if to hide his anguished expression. "There's been a change in the price of corn," he said. "They're only paying half last week's price. Even with everything else gone, there's still too much corn."

She watched him quietly for a moment before asking the question he would expect of her. "Will we make enough to last the winter?"

He swung a load of crates over his shoulder and began moving off toward the storage shed. "Ralph Thomas says he plowed his corn under this year and planted barley, but the corn came up anyway." He moved slowly, his back bent, his head lowered. He resembled an aging burro. "Seems people didn't have much choice about their crops this year. Everybody's growin' corn."

She took a crate in each hand and tagged along behind him. "There's something strange about the corn. I don't just mean its growing while everything else is dead. It's something else. I tried to tear it away from the fence and . . . and it just wouldn't be destroyed. I couldn't tear off a single leaf."

He was stacking the empty crates beside the shed, keeping them ready for morning, a new day of picking. "You never was too strong," he teased.

She knew he was laughing at her; not maliciously, but in that quiet, lovable way of his he was attempting to joke away her fears.

"But I would have thought all these years would have given you a better grip than that." When he straightened up from his task, the expression on his face was slightly altered, a forced smile playing about his cracked lips. "Women," he said hopelessly.

Before she could protest, he had picked up his hoe and was moving off toward the endless rows of corn. With a final look of apprehension, she turned and went back into the house.

After dinner, Jack lit his pipe and settled back in his old leather chair to wait for the evening news. Dorothy cleared the table and washed the dishes with as little water as possible. Leaning against the drain, she stared out of the window above the sink.

There was a full moon and not a cloud in the sky. The cornfields were bathed in a silver half-light, and although there was no wind, the stalks seemed to be moving. It could have been her imagination, or it could have been the heat. Sometimes the heat rising from the ground gave the impression of movement. To satisfy herself, she went to the screen door and stuck her head out to peer across the fields.

The familiar voice of the newscaster filled the house behind her:

No relief in sight for Californians. The fiercest heat wave in the country's history continues to halt operations of the metropolitan cities.

No relief, she repeated to herself. And the corn goes on growing as if everything were normal.

The reservoirs are at critical capacity. The Sacramento authorities have announced the suspension of all shipping until the depth of the river is safe enough to accommodate river traffic. The danger of vessels going aground has increased alarmingly.

The newscaster's voice droned on endlessly with a repetition of the news they had heard for the past few weeks. Dorothy let the screen door slam. She came back to the drain and raked scraps into Queenie's dish. She carried it out onto the porch and called the dog, her voice unable to compete with the volume of the radio.

Several reports have been received from the Fresno area of deaths caused by heat. Speculations of mass hysteria have been forwarded to all law enforcement offices. Several reports of hallucinations have come into the station from the Los Banos farm belt. Farmers are claiming peculiarities in their corn crop. One family—

The radio sputtered, then was silent. Jack had probably thought she was listening and had not wanted her to hear anything about the corn that would make her react as she had that morning.

The silence following the switching off of the radio was quickly filled by a strange, hypnotic buzzing that was unlike

195

anything she had ever heard before. It vaguely resembled the night song of crickets mingled with a whisper of wind; but she had already satisfied herself that there was no wind. And this year there had been no crickets—or mosquitoes, or any other pesky insects, now that she stopped to think about it.

Then the sight of Queenie's body made her scream, and Jack hurried from the house so quickly that he must have been poised, expecting her summons. The dog's lifeless body lay just outside the gate, her white fur matted with blood from deep slashes. One slash had opened the veins of her throat, but she had managed to drag herself home across the cornfields. She had reached the gate without the strength to cross the narrow yard.

Jack was still bent over the dog when Dorothy suddenly grabbed him by the arm.

"Listen! It's getting louder!"

He looked up at her, the moonlight reflected in his eyes. His hand, lying on Queenie's body, was covered with blood. "What's getting louder?" he asked in a broken voice.

"Don't you hear it? Listen!"

Crouched beside the dog, his head cocked, he listened to the strange sound. Then he rose and stared out toward the fields. "When did it start?"

"I noticed it when you turned off the radio."

After a moment, he said: "The radio went dead. A battery most likely."

"It was low at first. Almost like crickets from the irrigation ditches."

"Probably the ground crackin' from the heat," he reasoned.

Unconvinced, she moved closer to him and put her arm through his. "It sounds like things dying," she said. "All sorts of things dying at the same time."

He pushed her gently away, embarrassed by her womanly fright. "Go inside," he told her. "I've got to bury Queenie."

He walked back to the porch and bent down to the open area under it, where he kept his tools. He fumbled about in the dark, finally bringing out the scythe and rake and leaning them against the house before he found the spade. She stood staring around the yard nervously, suddenly afraid of the outside but unwilling to leave her husband alone. When he came back with the spade, she took it from him while he lifted the dog's body onto his shoulder. When he moved off toward the ditch, she was close at his heels.

After Queenie had been buried, they came back to the house without speaking. He walked slowly, with his head down on his chest. She was unable to find any words of comfort for the loss of his beloved dog. The sound had stopped, she had noticed, but she did not mention it to him. Whatever it had been, the earth cracking from the heat or some strange insect, it was now silent and she was thankful.

Jack washed away the blood and went directly to bed. Later when she joined him, he mumbled, "Who would have wanted to do that to Queenie? She was a good dog."

"It's the Lord's will," she said with a sigh. "It's not for us to understand what things live and what things have to die."

"I reckon that's so." He rolled over on his side and was asleep before she had even closed her eyes.

She lay still, looking about the moonlit room, thinking: *Is that so? Would the Lord let everything except the corn die off?* She let her hand travel over to the bedside table. It groped about the open shelf until it settled on the dusty Bible. She let it rest there for a long moment before retracting it.

Maybe, she thought, *it was the Russians doing something to the crops. With all those things they were hearing on the radio lately, it was possible.* She wondered if anyone else had thought of this. Or was it the farmers' fault? It was true that they had pushed the land, not letting the fields lie idle because of the need for profit. Tomorrow she would mention these things to Jack. She would be able to tell by his reaction if he had had the same thoughts.

She closed her eyes and drifted into the sleep of the exhausted.

Dorothy turned and looked at Jack. He was sleeping soundly, his face white in the moonlight streaming through the window above his head.

Something had wakened her, something unfamiliar to the sounds of the night. She raised herself to her elbows, listening.

It came again—the sound of something tearing through wood.

She slipped her feet over the edge of the bed, and lit the lamp. Then, cautiously, she moved to the doorway and peered into the dimness of the living room. The noise seemed to have come from the kitchen. She could see the silhouetted pattern of her floral curtains against the kitchen window. Reaching around the frame of the door, she flicked the light switch and the blinding glare filled the room. She moved closer to the kitchen door, and hesitated. The kitchen light was turned on near the outside door, across the room. The moonlight, although it was bright, did not penetrate the curtains enough to illuminate the cluttered area.

As her eyes became accustomed to the darkness, what she saw turned her blood cold. She fell back against the frame of the door, slid to the floor, and lay there screaming.

A stalk of corn had torn its way through the floorboards. It was reaching, twisting its way toward the faucets. Her screams caused it to pause like a being with a sense of hearing, to examine her crumpled form as one examines an adversary. It swung out at her, fell short of her legs and struck the floor.

She could hear Jack stumbling about in the back room, calling her name in his confusion. If she waited, he would come and destroy the corn; but the sight of the stalk slashing out at her brought back the fury of her resentment. She struggled to her feet, moaning like a wild animal, and fumbled for the knife rack on the wall. Then she charged toward the swaying plant, screaming and slashing wildly with the butcher knife.

When Jack reached her, she was sitting on the floor, stabbing at the base of the stalk.

The upper part had been severed and lay twitching like a slaughtered chicken.

"I knew it," she cried. "All the time I knew it was the corn!"

The look of utter horror on his face dispelled her hysteria.

"We're lost," she moaned. "We are all of us lost." She buried her face in her arms and lay sobbing while he moved around the room closing windows and doors over the screens, sliding bolts into place.

"Hurry, woman!" was all he said as he dashed past her into the other rooms.

She staggered to her feet, following through the house behind him, doing no more than watching him slide pieces of furniture against the doors.

The splintering had begun again in the kitchen. The corn was tearing away the floorboards. It would only be a matter of time before the house belonged to the corn. The hypnotic buzzing had also begun again: it surrounded the house, and intoned like a dirge on their ears.

Dorothy ran to the window and pulled back the curtains.

The yard had been entirely claimed. The corn stood swaying in the moonlight like a field of slithering snakes. From the far corner of the valley came a red glow, almost as intense as a sunrise.

"It must be happening everywhere!" she screamed at Jack. "They're burning the corn!"

In the moment just before the lights went out, she saw jack running into the kitchen wielding a hatchet.

"It's got the wires!" he shouted. She could hear the hatchet striking something solid, something that fell heavily to the floor.

"We've got to burn it!" she cried out hysterically. "Like the others! We've got to burn the corn! All of it! It's our only hope!"

She was already taking the kerosene lanterns from their place above the mantel. He came and took them from her, lit the wicks and stood staring at her, the yellow glow illuminating his stricken face.

"The house will go, too," he said, his voice low, almost lacking any expression. He could have been telling her the fields had been plowed, or the chickens fed. Only the terror in his eyes belied his voice. A dark, swollen welt across his neck where the corn must have slashed him had begun to fleck with rich, dark blood.

There was a rumble of movement beneath their feet; the house seemed to groan as if from the force of an earthquake.

"Get sheets," he told her. "Twist them together and tie them in knots. Hurry!"

She ran into the bedroom and tore the sheets from the bed, twisting them into tight balls and carrying them back to where he was crouched on the floor in the flickering light of the lanterns.

He doused the sheets with kerosene.

"Now soak your gown from the faucet. Soak it good. And tie something around your head."

While he prepared the torches, she went back into the kitchen, staying clear of the dead corn and broken floorboards. The water came from the tap in a weak stream. The corn's roots must have been choking the pipes, draining away the water and increasing its strength for the attack.

She soaked her gown and hair, and then filled a pail, carrying it back to where her husband stood waiting. He bent while she poured the water over him. Then, dripping like a drowned pup, he picked up the sheets and kerosene lanterns and moved toward the door.

"Stay close behind me," he warned her. "If somethin' happens . . ."

He kicked the chest away from the door, and they moved out onto the porch to face the corn.

The buzzing increased when they came into view. Huddled close behind Jack, her hands pressed over her ears, Dorothy stared at the corn, and at her yard, now the domain of the corn.

"Burn it!" she screamed. "Burn it!"

Jack touched the flame to one of the sheets. As it flared up, he tossed it into the middle of the yard. It hit and exploded, the flames licking up the stalks of corn, leaping from one to the other, each stalk bursting with a crackle as it was consumed by fire.

"We've got to reach the boulder!" he yelled at her; and she nodded her understanding. "Along the road! The corn's scarcest there!"

He lit the second sheet and flung it far out past the first. Then they waited for the flame directly along the walk to subside enough so that they could pass.

The sound of splintering glass came from inside the house. The house now belonged to the corn. Their only safe refuge, the tiny porch, was being licked by flames. They must make their run for the boulder. They must make it soon, or never.

Jack reached for the scythe leaning against the house, braced it firmly under his right arm and gripped the handle with knuckle-whitening force. He pulled her to his left side, close to his body, the pressure of his fingers digging into the flesh of her arm. The glow of the fire reflected on his face, revealing the hard set of his jaw, his eyes defying the corn to block their escape.

"Now!" he yelled, and he pulled her forward off the porch into the inferno of the yard.

Her face was pressed into the curve of his arm. She ran blindly, her legs obeying every movement of his body, stumbling with the force of his sweeps with the scythe, and leaping to the command of his grip. At times her feet did not seem to touch the ground. She seemed to be carried along by a running giant whose one arm possessed enough strength to balance her at his side as if she were no more than a weightless doll.

Then their pace slowed, and she opened her eyes. They had reached the road where only a few stalks of corn blocked their way. Jack moved ahead of her, his powerful arms wielding the scythe in their defense. He cleared their path to the boulder, and then half lifted, half threw her up its side. She grasped the sharp crags of the rock, pulling herself steadily upward until she lay panting in the bowl of its concave top. He crawled in beside her, and they peered over the rim.

They watched the destruction of the valley until morning, until the sun rose hot and red above the lingering blanket of smoke.

"Come," Jack said. He took her by the arm and they climbed down from the boulder.

On the ground once again, Jack stood absently shuffling his toe through the blackened soil. Then he drew her protectively into the curve of his body, lay his head gently over the top of her gray head. Without looking back to where their farm had stood, they moved off slowly down the dirt road.

Tiny green sprouts of corn had begun to force their way up through the blackened fields.